W

"I am nothing—
if not an honorable man."

Tray Hampton quickly raised himself
up from the spot where he and Ruth
had been lying on the meadow grass.
He stared down at her, his eyes
clouding with sadness.

Everything had been so right—
absolutely, perfectly right. What could
have happened to change things?
Ruth sat up shakily and stared at his
bowed head. "I don't understand...."

"What we were about to do was
dishonorable." His face was open,
totally vulnerable.

"For whom?" she demanded. "Don't
try to tell me you were saving the fair
damsel's honor."

He turned to her with a smile of bitter
irony. "But that's precisely what I was
doing. Only in this case, the fair
damsel happens to be another
woman—the one I've promised to
marry. So you see, what almost
happened between us would have
been most unfair."

"If you mean that," she said urgently,
"then what you're doing now is more
unfair. To us, *and* to her."

MELINDA CROSS would love her readers to believe she was kidnapped as a child by an obscure nomadic tribe and rescued by a dashing adventurer. Actually, though, she is a wonderfully imaginative American writer who is married to a true romantic. Every spring, without fail, when the apple orchard blooms, her husband gathers a blanket, glasses and wine and leads Melinda out to enjoy the fragrant night air. Romantic fantasy? Nonsense, she says. This is the stuff of real life.

Books by Melinda Cross

HARLEQUIN PRESENTS
847—LION OF DARKNESS
889—A VERY PRIVATE LOVE

These books may be available at your local bookseller.

Don't miss any of our special offers. Write to us at the following address for information on our newest releases.

Harlequin Reader Service
901 Fuhrmann Blvd., P.O. Box 1397, Buffalo, NY 14240
Canadian address: P.O. Box 2800, Postal Station A,
5170 Yonge St., Willowdale, Ont. M2N 6J3

MELINDA CROSS

what's right

Harlequin Books

**TORONTO • NEW YORK • LONDON
AMSTERDAM • PARIS • SYDNEY • HAMBURG
STOCKHOLM • ATHENS • TOKYO • MILAN**

Harlequin Presents first edition September 1986
ISBN 0-373-10914-8

Original hardcover edition published in 1985
by Mills & Boon Limited

CHAPTER ONE

'PRIDE goeth before the fall, Ruth.'

She'd heard the expression a hundred times—no, a thousand times—and still she would not have changed a thing. Even now, the only thing that bothered her was that she hadn't fallen very far. She had hoped to be a great deal higher before she took her first tumble.

The pride had been with her always; a grim, unshakeable certainty that she had been blessed with beauty and talent, and that pretending she had neither would be pointless and self-defeating. Facts were facts, and denying them for the sake of false modesty was a peculiar human characteristic she had never been able to understand. Even as a child, in the barren farmhouse where poverty had stopped time a century before, Ruth had cherished stormy dreams of greatness she had never doubted lay in her future. 'I'll be famous one day, Mother,' she had piped with the confidence of youth, 'and then I'll buy you wonderful things.' Her mother had always smiled sadly, replying in that low, soft-spoken voice of hers that money bought nothing of value, and that piety, humility and reverence were the dreams Ruth should seek.

But piety, humility and reverence, qualities her mother possessed in abundance, had brought nothing but an early death to the overworked widow, and Ruth saw no value in that end at all. She was headstrong, determined, and absolutely impervious to the psychological ravages of deprivation. She knew her destiny lay far beyond the confines of the poverty and obscurity in which she had been raised, and she would settle for no less.

As she nursed her mother through the long, painful

illness that would ultimately cause her death, the deeply
lined, kind face would smile at her fondly, wondering
how her loins could have produced such a beautiful, yet
alien creature. In her last breath, the weakened woman
had touched the cascading waves of her daughter's
vibrant red hair, a colour that had always offended her
slightly, and spoke to her only child the legacy she had
as yet failed to impart. 'Pride goeth before the fall,
Ruth,' she murmured one last time, and then she had
died.

Ruth mourned her bitterly, knowing that the humility
had been genuine, and that in her own way, her mother
had been as true to herself as Ruth was to hers. For a
long time she regretted that she had not inherited a
measure of her mother's inexhaustible goodness, never
realising that she had.

After her mother's death she sold the farm, used the
proceeds to finance four years in a college that
purported to teach interior structural design, then
launched an assault on the city where all her dreams
were supposed to come true. She had devoted her future
to a career of designing perfect environments for
imperfect people, and never once considered the irony
in that.

She had known her own gifts, taken deep pride in
her abilities, and naively expected her worth to be
measured by such things. But now, at the age of
twenty-six, she was coming to the bitter realisation
that social skills often ranked above talent and ability
in the world of business. Her dreams were slipping
away; not because she was inept or unskilled, but
simply because she could not play by somone else's
rules.

She stood quietly at her desk, picturing her mother in
her mind's eye, and the rigid lines of her face softened,
revealing the breathtaking innocence of a woman who
had not yet learned to compromise values for
expedience.

'What are you doing, Ruth?'

She looked up sharply at the worried face in the doorway to her office. She stared at harmless, eager-to-please Sally, with her harmless, eager-to-please looks, and wondered if that was what you had to become to make it in this world: an affable, non-threatening personality who pleased all of the people all of the time.

'I'm packing up, Sally,' she answered, a little more harshly than she had intended. She threw one more file folder into the box on her desk, then relented when she saw hurt creep into the mournful brown eyes. 'Sorry. I didn't mean to bark. Harold just gave me the axe, and I don't think I'm taking it very well.'

'What! He fired you? He can't!'

Ruth paused in her packing to laugh, pleased that she could still manage the effort. Sally always sounded like a little girl when she got excited; snapping out short, hysterical sentences in a childishly high voice.

'Of course he can, Sally. It's his company now.'

'But you're the best designer we've got; the only designer worth mentioning, and he knows it! You were here long before he was, and look at the accounts you've brought in just since he came! Waverlys, and the Hampton House—my God, I forgot. Who'll finish the Hampton House if you go?'

Ruth sagged into her chair and ran both hands through the thick red mane that framed her face. She knew the gesture would cost her the perfectly coiffed, professional image she'd tried to preserve all morning, but she didn't care anymore. She wouldn't be meeting the client anyway. 'The Hampton designs are finished,' she sighed. 'And that, by the way, is why I got fired.'

'But they were wonderful!' Sally protested. 'Even Harold liked them. He said so himself.'

'So he did,' Ruth answered, dropping her chin into the cup of her palm.

'Well, it's professional suicide!' Sally snapped, and

Ruth looked up at her even-tempered assistant with mild surprise. Displays of temper were totally out of character for Sally. 'Well it is!' the younger woman defended her anger. 'By firing you, Harold Westchester is destroying his own company, and I'm going to tell him so! Right now!'

She stomped out of the office in a huff, and Ruth leaned back in her chair tiredly, grateful for the solitude.

There were a million things to think about. Packing, leaving the office, facing a future painfully empty without her work—she had to think about all those things. But for the moment, she would rest. There would be more than enough time for thinking later.

She put her head down on her desk and closed her eyes, picturing the Hampton House drawings in her mind. She had lived with them, day and night, for so long she could hardly imagine life without them. They had become master of her time, consuming her thoughts and her dreams, obsessing her with a passion that excluded everything else. Too much passion, she thought. Too much pride. She had given too much of herself to that ghastly, sprawling mansion; and now that she knew she would never see it again, that she would never see the weeks become reality, she felt drained; totally empty. How long had it been since that project had become the force that drove her; the primary reason for her existence? Three weeks? Four? Had it only been that long?

She forced herself to remember that morning Westchester had called her into his office, that straining paunch of his fairly quivering with excitement.

'We have a chance for a big one, Ruth. The chance of a lifetime, in fact.' He had announced it sonorously, giving each word the impact of a royal proclamation. 'The Hampton House. There isn't a design studio in the country that wouldn't kill for this account, and *he came to us*! It's worth a fortune on its own, not to mention the new business it would send our way. Hampton saw

the Waverly place, and wants the same designer to submit drawings.'

'Hampton?' she had asked, drawing a total blank on the name.

'Tray Hampton, of course! You *do* know who he is, don't you?'

She had shrugged and shaken her head.

'My God, Ruth! Sometimes I think you live in a cave! How many times have I told you? You must learn who the movers are in this city! Read the society pages; watch the news; do your homework! You have to *woo* people in our business. Accounts like this don't fall out of the sky, you know.'

'Really?' She had raised her eyebrows a fraction of an inch. 'I thought Hampton came to us because he saw our work at Waverly's. That's the only kind of "wooing" I can manage, Harold. Sorry.'

His fat jowls had trembled with the force of his clenched jaw. 'Sometimes I wonder what Father was thinking of when he took you in,' he had said testily. 'You just don't have the team spirit it takes to survive in this world.'

'And neither did he, Harold, as you have good cause to know. He despised the "team spirit" you talk about so much. He built this company on his own, with no team, no wooing, nothing but his own talents, and he did rather well, don't you think?'

'But nobody *liked* him,' Harold had protested in a voice dangerously close to a whine.

'Nevertheless they came to him. All of them. He was the best interior designer in the city—maybe the country—and that made him rich. That made him successful. Not reading the society pages.'

Harold had plopped his bulk into the chair his father had occupied for years, and fastened a malevolent stare on Ruth. She hated him when he looked like that. His little eyes seemed to drill right through her, as if he could control her thoughts by the simple act of looking vicious.

'Well Father's dead,' he had hissed, 'and Westchester Design is mine now, and it's going to be run my way. You're either part of the team, or you're out on the street. Now which is it going to be?'

She had sighed at the empty threat and shook her head. Harold would no more fire her than she would quit. They needed each other too much. He needed her to create the designs the world had come to expect from Westchester; and she needed him for an outlet for her work. The work is everything, she had reminded herself silently. You must be able to work, because without it, life is meaningless. Dealing with men like Harold is a small price to pay for the chance to see your designs brought to life. He's a nuisance, that's all. A bothersome fly to be brushed away so you can get on with more important things.

But there was more than that; another reason she tolerated the petulant, childish control Harold insisted on exercising every now and then, just to keep his hand in. Her loyalty to his father lingered. Still, almost six months after his death, she served her first master. Perhaps the only master she would ever have. Her debt to Westchester Design, and to the incredible man who had made it, held her captive even now.

She had composed the features that always betrayed her feelings too readily, and had looked Harold directly in the eye. 'All right, Harold. When do I meet Mr Hampton?'

'You don't.'

'What? I can't design the interior of a house for a person I don't know! That's part of it; you know it is! We make the home fit the owner. That's what Westchester Design is all about!'

His little cupid mouth had turned up in a smug crescent. He enjoyed making eveything as difficult as possible. 'Not this time. Mr Hampton's instructions were very specific. You'll be permitted free run of the house, of course; but the plans are to be your own. No

imput from him whatsoever. Two other firms are submitting drawings and bids under the same terms. The company whose drawings he selects will win the contract.'

'That's an impossible task!' she had spluttered. 'How can I begin to guess what the man would like when I haven't even met him?'

Harold had barely been able to disguise his pleasure in seeing her lose control, but he had made his voice stern. 'Oh, Ruth, stop complaining. *I* haven't even met the man. He doesn't see anyone he doesn't have to, and when you're Tray Hampton, that includes almost everyone. I suggest you do a little research on him, and try to work from that. If you'd been doing your homework all along, you wouldn't have to take the time now. But . . .' his smile had widened unpleasantly, '. . . we do have an edge on the competition. He liked the Waverly house, remember.'

He had tossed a large manila envelope towards her across the desk. 'Directions to the house are in there, and the key. It's empty now, so you can view it whenever you like. He just bought the place, and refuses to set foot inside until the interior is finished.' He laid a chubby hand on the gloss of the massive desk, and toyed with one of his rings. 'Be grateful you don't have to work with him, Ruth. From what I hear, the man's a tyrant.'

'How much time do I have?'

'One month. He'll be here at 10:00 a.m. sharp, April first.'

Ruth had taken a deep breath and had held it until she had felt her temper reduce to a slow simmer. 'What's the budget?' she had asked finally.

Harold had leant back in his chair slowly and had delivered his answer with an almost lascivious relish. 'There isn't one. *Carte blanche*. Tray Hampton never needed a budget in his life.'

She had opened the manila envelope later, alone in

her car, contemptuously tossing aside the pages of biography on Hampton Harold had included, looking for the directions to the house. They had been drawn carefully—by a draftsman, no doubt—on an expensive sheet of buff bond imprinted with the Hampton Enterprises logo. But suddenly the directions became meaningless, because on the bottom of the sheet, a message had been scrawled carelessly in the black, forceful slashes of a felt pen, and the slashes had snatched her attention and held it, and she couldn't pull her gaze away. 'April 1—10:00 a.m.—J.T.H.3.'

She had stared at the words without blinking until her vision blurred, moved beyond all reason by the simple, thoughtless marks a man had made on a piece of paper. There was arrogance in the script, and anger, and evidence of the driving force of a man who demanded precision and perfection, and got both. Always. It was the impatient, bold, forward scrawl of a man of unlimited power, and she had touched the words tentatively with one finger, feeling his presence like a tangible thing, trembling at the sensation.

She had dropped the paper to her lap then, throwing her head back against the seat and emitting a nervous little laugh.

Don't be stupid, Ruth, she had chided herself. There isn't a man alive who could be half of what that handwriting implies. There was only one, and he's dead. Besides, a clerk probably wrote that.

Her eyes had flown wide and she had scrambled through the biography sheets, searching for the first page. She had found it, held it with trembling fingers, and read the first line.

His full name was Jonathan Terrence Hampton III. J.T.H.3. The initials were his.

She had opened her fingers and let the sheet flutter unnoticed to the floor, while she had stared straight ahead, her eyes fixed on a point far in the distance. She didn't have to read further. The biography was meaningless now. She already knew Jonathan Terrence Hampton III—intimately—from his handwriting on the bottom of a page, and the interiors she designed would be for that man, and no other.

She had known then it would be the most important work of her life, and had shuddered.

And that had been the beginning.

She had visited the house, wondered what the man who belonged to that handwriting could ever see in such a mediaeval monstrosity, and had shrugged her doubts away. No matter that the exterior was a poor imitation of the old Rhine castles; tedious, unimaginative and forbidding. The inside would be his. She would make it his, and when he saw her drawings, he would know it.

For the first time in her life, she had understood the old expression 'labour of love', and had become emotionally closer each day to a man she had never met. With bold slashes of her marking pen she had ravaged the interior elevations, knocking out a wall in one room, raising the ceiling in another, widening gloomy hallways, opening the entire house to light and air and space. She had worked long into the nights, forgetting to eat or sleep, obsessed by the challenge of creating an environment worthy of the man her imagination had spawned. She had visited the house again and again, touching the mantles, the walls, the bannisters; thinking that he had touched them, that his hand had rested where hers did now, and then feeling the tremulous thrill such a thought produced.

The effort had totally drained her, both emotionally and physically, but at the end of the month, she had known she had achieved not only the best she could do, but the best anyone could have done. The pride had been overwhelming, but she had savoured it for only a short time before she had heard that gentle voice from the past whispering, 'Pride goeth before the fall, Ruth,' then a sick, deep despair had consumed her. She had controlled it long enough to trace her initials lightly on each finished drawing, then she had slumped over her board and had sobbed, thin shoulders quaking with the force of it, for a very long time.

It had been a devastating, unwelcome revelation: that although the house would be worthy of the man, no man could ever be worthy of the house. She had succumbed to an image her mind had created, becoming so obsessed with the fantasy that reality could never hope to match it. With the work completed, the fantasy dissolved, and the imaginary man who had given her life meaning for the last four weeks had simply ceased to exist. There were no such men in the world anymore. The world would not allow them to survive. Martin Westchester had been the last, and he was dead.

'Ruth?' Sally's voice called timidly from the doorway. 'Ruth? Are you asleep?'

She raised her head with an effort and straightened in her chair. 'No, Sally. Just daydreaming. Come on in.'

'I can't even get near Westchester's office,' Sally complained, sinking into the chair opposite Ruth's desk. 'He left strict orders that he wasn't to be disturbed before Hampton arrived. But his secretary said he's setting up your drawings, so he still plans on using them. I don't understand, Ruth. What happened in there?'

'My drawings were fine, Sally. It was the one he added that caused the blow-up.'

'The one *he* added? Harold Westchester, who can't even walk a straight line, let alone draw one? *He* submitted a drawing?'

'No, no. The client did.' Ruth closed her eyes slowly. 'It came by messenger last night. Apparently Hampton wanted to re-do the foyer with his own ideas, so he sent over his own drawing, and Harold substituted it for mine. But you know how it is, Sally. The entrance to any building says everything—it sets the standards for the rest.'

'So?'

'So it was trash!' she exploded. 'Pretentious, unadulterated trash! Not even original trash; but copies of a hundred other ideas all clashing together into one horrible whole!' She took a deep breath and blew it out through her lips. 'So I refused to keep it as part of the exhibit, and to make certain it wouldn't be, I ripped it in half.'

Sally's eyebrows shot up and her mouth formed a silent whistle. 'You tore up a client's drawing?' she gasped. 'Right in front of Harold?'

'I did,' Ruth said firmly. 'And I'd do it again. It's the most responsible thing I've done in weeks. That foyer had no place in my house.'

She blushed quickly, realising her words had implied ownership, but Sally merely nodded in understanding.

'It was the best thing you've done, Ruth,' she said quietly. 'It was worth trying to protect.'

Ruth stared intently at the younger woman, surprised by the depth of her perception. She had underestimated Sally. It was a mistake she made too often with people. 'Thank you, Sally,' she whispered. 'I didn't expect anyone to understand that.'

'So what will you do now?'

'Find work. Somewhere. Anywhere. I have to work.'

Sally blinked once, pursing generous lips into a circle of determination. 'Call when you can afford to take on an assistant,' she said simply. 'I'm a bargain, you know. When you're in the market for one of those, I'll be here.'

'A bargain is the least of what you are,' Ruth smiled. 'I'll keep in touch.'

It took only a few moments to pack the rest of her belongings. She was almost finished when she heard Harold greet Mr Hampton in the outer office, his voice oozing servility. The temptation was strong to peer around the doorframe; to catch just a glimpse of the man who had been such a great part of her life for the last month; but she quashed the impulse by remembering the drawing of the foyer. The man who had compiled that garish piece of tastelessness was not worth seeing. She felt bitterly betrayed that the man had not matched his handwriting; and foolish for thinking he ever could. Eventually she heard the door to Harold's private office click shut, and the sound made her shudder with revulsion. Her soul lay exposed on the drawings within that room, and she had displayed it thoughtlessly, foolishly, to a man who would never be able to understand the gesture.

Ten minutes later she was walking down the wide hallway that led away from the offices of Westchester Design, carrying a box too large for the few possessions she had chosen to take with her.

There should be a band, she thought, or better yet, the keening wail of mourners; *something* to mark her departure from a place that had been her life for the last five years. But the silence was absolute as she approached the elevators, and for the millionth time in the last six months, she wished Martin were still alive.

'Miss Lyons!'

She stopped dead at the sound of her name, and felt her eyes widen until a circle of white surrounded the brilliant green irises. But it wasn't her name that stopped her. It was the voice. It reverberated imperiously in the empty corridor, with the deep ring of an authority that never expects to be questioned. It paralysed her with the bright, cutting sound of confidence she had heard in a man's voice only once before, and she stood there helplessly, afraid to move and shatter the spell; afraid to even turn around, for fear she would find no one there.

'You *are* Miss Lyons, aren't you? I can't imagine two women in one building with hair quite that colour.'

It had spoken again, closer now, right behind her, so it must be real. She turned slowly, tightening her grip on the pathetic pasteboard box, and looked up into eyes cold with the colour of a stormy sea.

She saw nothing but the eyes. No face, no body, and now, in the silence, there was no voice. Only the eyes. They belonged to the man in her head, the man she had fabricated from a few scrawled words; and she was so astonished to find they were real that she couldn't speak. They were piercing and arrogant, and sceptically inquisitive, as though looking for something they were certain could never be found.

'Well? *Are* you Miss Lyons?' the voice demanded, and the eyes narrowed impatiently.

'Yes,' she said softly, barely moving her lips. 'I am.'

'The same Miss Lyons who tore my foyer in half?'

She closed her eyes and breathed deeply, remembering. Forget the eyes, she commanded herself. Forget the voice. Forget the dream. He designed the foyer. Remember that.

'The same,' she replied, more strongly now, and turned back towards the elevators without looking at him again.

'Good. We'll start at the house tomorrow. I have an hour free in the morning. Arrange to be there by eight.'

Her lips curved in a bitter smile as she stabbed at the lift button. 'I'm afraid you don't understand, Mr Hampton,' she said steadily, her gaze fastened on the lift door 'I won't be handling your account.' She stepped through the doors when they parted and turned, expecting to find him facing her from the hallway. Her last words would be said just before the doors closed in his face. It was the kind of dramatic exit she loved.

'Of course you will.' The voice came from right next to her left ear, and she jumped just as the doors sighed shut. 'There are a few minor changes I'd like to make, otherwise your plans are ... well, we'll talk about your plans tomorrow.'

Just turning to face him required more courage than

she could muster at the moment. She was too depleted from the month's labours, too shaken by the events of the morning, to square off against another disappointment. She didn't want to see, and be forced to admit, how different he was from the man of her fantasy.

'Mr Hampton,' she said evenly, still staring straight ahead at the blank door, 'it's perfectly clear that you're not a man who accepts contradiction gracefully, but I repeat: I will not be handling your account; nor will I be implementing my designs for that monstrosity you purchased.'

She didn't expect the deep chuckle, nor the firm hand on her elbow when the doors parted at street level, propelling her towards the dark recesses of the building's ground floor restaurant.

'Now just a minute!' she protested, bracing her feet ineffectively against the insistent thrust forward.

'No need to panic, Miss Lyons. I'm not abducting you. We're just going to have a cup of coffee together, that's all.'

'I don't have time for coffee. I have things to do . . .'

'Don't be ridiculous!' the voice snapped. 'You've just been fired. What could you possibly have to do? Table for two, please,' he instructed the hostess, keeping a firm grip on her elbow. And then in an aside to her, 'We'll see how long you can avoid looking at me when we're seated directly across from one another.'

She felt her cheeks flush a furious red, and heard the answering amusement in his tone. 'Your face is very nearly the colour of that preposterous hair of yours. Now sit down and try to compose yourself. Two coffees, Miss. Black.'

She jerked her eyes up to look at him then, enraged by his patronising manner. She was fully prepared to spit out an angry retort, level him with a disdainful glare, then leave him alone and embarrassed at the small table.

But none of that happened. When her eyes connected

with his, the strength drained immediately from her legs, and they lost the ability to support her. She sagged into the chair, still clutching the ridiculous cardboard box, her eyes wide and her lips slightly parted.

'Well! Eye contact at last. I was beginning to think I was herding a zombie. Now put down that pathetic box you've been clutching like the crown jewels and make an attempt at conversation, will you? I have no time for games this morning, and frankly, you're trying my patience.'

She knew he was saying something that should make her indignant, but the words barely registered in her mind. She was vaguely aware of staring at him intently, but couldn't stop herself.

He was the man in her head. The man she had imagined. And although she had never really put a face to that fantasy creature, if she had, it would have been his. Still, had she been asked at that moment to describe him, she would have been unable to comply. Although she saw the sweep of blond hair that angled over his brow, the purposeful slash of a mouth across a strong, clean-shaven chin, it was the eyes that captivated her, that dominated the face, hinting at the keen intelligence behind them, and that was all she could have described.

'Really, Miss Lyons,' he said with amusement. 'First you refused to look at me at all, and now you won't stop . . . Ah, thank you, Miss. Here.' He tapped the cup the waitress had set in front of her with one finger. 'Drink up, and then tell me why it is you won't be supervising the make-over of what you referred to as my monstrosity.'

She focused on the rim of her coffee cup. 'If you know I've been fired, you know the answer to that already,' she replied evenly. 'My designs belong to Westchester. They were produced while I was employed by the company, therefore they belong to the company.'

'Spare me the legalities, Miss Lyons. I'm well aware of them. That's why I purchased the rights.'

'What?'

He shook his head once in irritation. 'I wanted the designs, so I bought them. It's that simple. Now they're mine, and I want the person who created them to supervise the actual work. Can you start tomorrow?'

'Harold would never sell those designs,' she protested in wonder. 'Especially if he knew you wanted them.'

He made a sound of contempt. 'The Harolds of this world will sell anything, Miss Lyons, if the price is right. What I can't understand is how Westchester Design achieved the reputation it has with that man at the helm. It's almost inconceivable that such incompetence should succeed.'

'It wasn't Harold,' she interjected quietly, looking past his face to a point in her mind. 'It was his father, Martin Westchester. He died a short time ago.'

He put his chin in his hand and stared at her thoughtfully. 'You surprise me, Miss Lyons. I would have thought the person who created those designs would have too much character to indulge in hero-worship; or was it more than that?'

She flashed a silent question at him with narrowed eyes.

'Your expression,' he explained with a curt nod. 'I've never seen such blatant adulation—for a dead man, no less.'

She stood so quickly that her chair rocked on its legs. 'He *was* a hero, Mr Hampton. One of the last. And if adulation was what you saw in my face, he earned it. Now if you'll excuse me . . .'

He snatched her wrist without changing position in his chair. 'You'd better sit down, Miss Lyons,' he said with a thin smile. 'You can't afford the luxury of indignation at the moment. I'll try to avoid insulting dead gods in the future, but if I should slip, you'll just have to overlook it. I don't really need you that much, you know; but without me, you're unemployed.'

'I'll find work, Mr Hampton!' she shot back. 'I've

managed without your patronage for quite some time now, and I'm sure I can continue to do so!'

'And I'll find another designer to implement your drawings,' he said smoothly. 'I'm sure no one else would object to incorporating the foyer you hated so much into your other plans . . .'

'You can't!' she breathed, dropping immediately back to her seat. 'You can't possibly use that foyer plan—not if you really like the rest of my work.'

He released her wrist and leaned back in his chair, a smile playing at the corners of his mouth. 'There's only one way for you to prevent it.'

She breathed deeply, trying to contain the frustration, feeling her nostrils flare with the effort. 'And if I agree? If I supervise the renovation?'

'Creative licence will be yours.'

'And the foyer?' she insisted.

He shrugged impatiently. 'Forget the foyer. Use your own design. Westchester wouldn't show it to me, but I'm sure it's spectacular.'

'It is,' she said simply, and he laughed out loud. It was a wonderful laugh, full of unbridled pleasure, released for the satisfaction of its owner, and no other. Her answering smile was automatic.

'I think we'll get along, Miss Lyons. Be at the house at eight tomorrow morning.' He stood quickly and tossed some bills on the table. 'And you may as well know from the start, I don't like to be kept waiting.'

'I knew that weeks ago,' she replied, looking directly up into his eyes, if only to prove to herself that she could do it.

His brows lifted slightly, then he turned and left her sitting there, staring at nothing.

CHAPTER TWO

RUTH and her smile had been strangers for so long that wearing it made her feel a little foolish. She had spent the best part of an hour trying to recapture the customary dignity of her solemn features, yet even as her car topped the rise that first gave view to the Hampton house, she felt the smile creep back again. The morning was full of anticipated promise, as if the world were holding its breath, and there was no way she could keep that anticipation from showing on her face.

The emotional roller coaster she had ridden for the last twenty-four hours had opened her to a variety of feelings she had not experienced in months. Part of her had died with Martin Westchester six months before, and there had been moments when she'd wondered if she would ever feel anything again.

But there's life in the old girl yet, she thought with a wry smile. She'd lost her job, and in the losing, had learned just how important her work was to her. There was still something worth fighting for, worth feeling for; and the blow at being suddenly unemployed was tempered by the astounding realisation that she still had the capacity to care.

But the surprise of that discovery had knocked away her defences, leaving her terribly vulnerable. Perhaps that was why she had been so susceptible to the undeniably charismatic presence of Tray Hampton.

She shouldn't have liked him. Under ordinary circumstances, she might not have. He was arrogant, patronising, irritable, and a dozen other things she found distasteful in other people, even though she knew she possessed many of these same characteristics herself. Worse yet, he had intuitively sensed her feelings

22

for Martin, and she resented the fact that he could read her so easily.

Still, he had at least made her feel anger. Even Harold, with all his stupidity, had not been able to accomplish that. And he had played her like a fish on a line, knowing full well that his threat to use the foyer plan she hated would force her to accept his offer of employment. She hated manipulative people, especially when she was the proposed object of their manipulations; yet in Hampton, the trait was not quite so despicable. For one thing, he had only coerced her into doing something she wanted desperately to do, and in an ironic way, she was grateful to him for giving her no choice. For another, the man appeared to be everything her imagination had conjured from his handwriting, with one glaring exception: the hideous foyer design. She had spent a restless night trying to match the man she had met with that mindless montage of other people's designs, and still could not associate the two. Either the man, or the drawing, was a lie. This morning she meant to discover which.

She pulled her car up behind a low-slung foreign model in the drive, and walked up the patterned flagstones towards the house. Because of the mass of shrubbery concealing the front entrance, Ruth didn't see Hampton until she nearly collided with him at the door.

She cried out as she jostled him and jumped back in surprise.

'Sorry,' he drawled. 'I didn't mean to startle you.'

She doubted the sincerity of that remark, sensing that this man would seek the advantage in any situation, the greatest of these being catching an opponent off-guard. One for your side, she thought to herself, and tempered her irritation when she spoke.

'It wasn't your fault,' she said, depriving him of the small victory of premeditation. 'It's this blasted entrance. It's less like a front door than anything I've ever seen, tucked away in the bushes like this. If the path didn't lead you right to it, you'd never know there was a door here at all.'

'I believe that was the intention when they designed mediaeval castles,' he said with a mocking smile. 'You didn't keep out the enemy with wide porches and welcome mats.'

'That's just the point,' she said irritably. 'Castles belong in medieaval Europe, not in twentieth-century rural America.'

He leaned back against the broad plank doors and grinned. 'It isn't exactly the house of your dreams, is it?'

'More like a nightmare,' she said without thinking, then grimaced, wishing she could take back the words. 'I'm sorry. That was a little too direct, even for me. It's the house of your dreams, and that's really all that matters.'

The force of his laugh brought him sharply erect. 'My God! Whatever gave you that idea?'

She looked up at him with a puzzled frown. 'You bought it, and I imagine you paid dearly for the privilege. You must love it.'

He shook his head with a peculiar half-smile and closed his eyes briefly. 'Things are not always as simple as they appear, Miss Lyons. You should learn to look beyond the obvious, and avoid jumping to conclusions. It'll put you in over your head one day.'

She pursed her lips thoughtfully, studying him, trying to make sense of what he said, and decided finally that he was only playing word games. His entire manner suggested insolent superiority, an attitude that was probably an asset in his world of big business, and a serious detriment to the development of any personal relationships. In his own way, he was as emotionally defensive as she was, and as inaccessible.

She smiled at that, thinking that they shared a common weakness, and wondered if she wore her façade as well as he did. Nothing in his appearance suggested any weakness whatsoever. This morning, for instance, he wore faded jeans and a denim shirt with the air of one who finds everyone else pitifully overdressed. In a flash of insight, she realised he could be wearing white tie and tails or a terry bathrobe, and still give the very same impression. It was an inbred gift, this ability to make everyone else feel somehow inadequate just by standing next to them, but Ruth possessed too much of it herself to be intimidated.

She made no attempt to conceal her scrutiny, and his eyes let her know he was aware of her examination, and welcomed it.

'You're really quite a snob, you know,' she smiled.

'And in that, at least, I think you may be my equal.'

She inclined her head and tensed slightly as his gaze wandered insolently over her body. She had dressed in jeans and a bulky sweater against the chill of an early spring morning, but suddenly wished she had chosen something more formal.

'You seem to be inordinately interested in the way I'm dressed,' she said sarcastically, calling attention to his appraisal instead of shirking from it. 'Is something sticking out somewhere?'

'Nothing that shouldn't be,' he laughed, 'with the possible exception of the chip on your shoulder.' She frowned at that. 'You're just not what I expected, and the irony there, of course, is that I should have expected that. Most people dress to impress me, especially when I have something they want. I find it interesting that you didn't take the trouble.'

'I have absolutely no talent for public relations, Mr Hampton. I dress to suit myself and the circumstances, which in this case included banging around a dusty old mausoleum of a house. I see you dressed with the same thought in mind.'

He glanced down at his clothes in an afterthought. 'Oh. No, I have somewhere else to go afterwards,' he said absently. 'Actually, I haven't been in this place since the day I first saw it. That was more than enough for me. Masochism just isn't my style.'

'Now I really don't understand,' she frowned. 'You don't like this house at all, do you?'

'Very good, Miss Lyons.'

'Then why . . .'

'Shall we go in?' he interrupted her, turning quickly to unlock the enormous doors.

She followed him into an area immediately inside the door, large enough to contain her entire apartment, as gloomy and unwelcoming as any room could be.

'The infamous foyer,' he said unnecessarily, closing the doors behind them.

Ruth wrinkled her nose at the dank smell of stone that permeated the entire house, and eyed the massive block walls with distaste. 'Why you thought marble and tapestry would enhance this dungeon is beyond me,' she murmured, almost to herself.

'Marble and tapestry?'

'The plan you sent over,' she explained.

His face darkened immediately, and suddenly she thought this house might be an appropriate background for him after all. He looked every bit as forbidding as the surroundings.

'I saw that drawing for the first time at your office yesterday morning,' he said sharply, 'and I certainly wasn't responsible for having it sent over.' He shook his head with an exasperated expression. 'My God. Marble and tapestry. Is that what it was? I barely glanced at it.'

She felt a brief surge of elation to learn that he and the drawing were unrelated, then remembered what that loathsome rendering had cost her. 'Harold fired me because he thought that plan was yours!' she accused him, but her display of temper brought only a slight lift of his brows.

'That was no fault of mine,' he said calmly.

'Of course it was! It came from Hampton Enterprises

by a Hampton messenger; or do you deny responsibility for the actions of people who use your name? And who was it, by the way?' she demanded. 'What demented moron conceived that abortion of taste and used your authority to present it?'

If her own expression was hostile, then his was deadly. 'I suggest you learn to control that temper of yours, Miss Lyons,' he said crisply, controlling his own very well, 'or you'll find yourself dismissed for the second time in twenty-four hours.'

She glared at him for a moment longer, then dropped her eyes in sullen acquiescence.

'Besides,' he said less vehemently, 'losing your job at Westchester is probably the best thing that could have happened to your career. A little publicity on what you do for me here, and the élite will be beating a path to your door. Your business will make Westchester look like a country store.'

All of her thoughts stopped at once. 'My business?'

'Of course. By the way, what will you call yourself? Something more imaginative than Lyons Design, I hope. Incidentally, you should incorporate immediately, before we sign any contracts, or the taxes will destroy your first profits.'

'You expect me to set up my own business on the strength of one job?'

'Oh, come now, Miss Lyons. Have a little more faith in the Hampton name. My recommendation will go a long way towards bringing you more business than you can handle—if you earn it, that is.'

She glowered at the implication that she might not, and he laughed at her.

'You certainly don't have much of a head for business, do you?' he chided. 'I suggest you find an assistant who does, or you'll be ruined before you start. Now come to the library, and we'll get the legalities over with. I'm running late already.'

She followed obediently through the narrow, echoing

corridors, her head swimming with the unexpected turns her life had taken in such a short time. She was on the threshhold of establishing her own studio—a dream she had entertained only in the most private recesses of her mind—and her first client was a man who evoked responses in her so long untouched she had thought they were dead.

By the time they seated themselves at the massive library table, she was numb to surprise, and could only nod stupidly at the various legal provisions he pointed out in a short, one-page contract.

'This is the fee Westchester intended to charge, so it's what I'll offer you,' he said, indicating an enormous sum in the last paragraph. 'Half now, the balance when the work is completed. Unless you'd care to bicker, of course.'

She shook her head silently, amazed at the size of the figure, rapidly calculating what could be done with it. It would pay her salary, and Sally's, for two years at least, buy a year's lease on the little building on Market Street she had covered, and provide for dozens of other amenities she hadn't expected from life for years to come.

'Silence is an unfamiliar condition for you, Miss Lyons. Is there something wrong?'

She glanced up from the contract and looked at him steadily, measuring her dreams against her principles. The latter won, and she sighed heavily. 'The figure is outrageous, Mr Hampton,' she said reluctantly.

He leaned on his hands, inclining his body across the table until his face was only inches from hers. 'All right,' he said carefully, 'but I warn you, I will go only so high. Try to tone down your avarice.'

She raised her brows in surprise, and then laughed with delight. 'No, no. You don't understand. It's too high already.'

He said nothing for a moment, and she could see from his expression that she had shocked him completely. 'Have you really had your head in the sand that long?' he asked finally. 'This is a fairly standard fee for this kind of contract. It was Westchester's bid, and of the three I solicited, his was low.'

She shook her head rapidly. 'If that's true, then every designer in the city is overpriced. It's a preposterous figure, especially since I'm a novice at this sort of thing.'

He straightened and smiled. 'Your principles are admirable, Miss Lyons, but they leave you terribly unsuited for the world of business. Besides, you're not a novice. You've been designing for Westchester for five years now. I checked. Almost every successful design that came out of that firm has been yours. Happily for you, I'm not buying your business acumen. I can see you're desperately short of that. I'm buying your creativity, and if I were you, I would consider that beyond price.'

'Thank you,' she whispered, dropping her eyes, knowing that that particular compliment, from this particular man, was the most valuable she had received since Martin's death.

'Don't thank me,' he said brusquely. 'I'm not responsible for your talent, and I don't dole out idle flattery. If you hear praise from me, it will be because you've earned it.' He brushed his hands together as if he had disposed of an extremely distasteful task. 'I'll have a bank draft for the first half delivered to you this afternoon, and my attorneys will call you about handling your incorporation. They should be able to push that through in short order, then we'll execute the contracts formally. Now let's get started. This was one room where I had a few changes to suggest.'

They toured the old castle together for nearly an hour while she took mental notes on his suggestions. For the most part, they were practical, not aesthetic; designed to accommodate his personal preferences for a larger bedroom, a more efficient kitchen complex, and security provisions absolutely essential for a man of his wealth.

The final change he requested involved a room originally designated as the conservatory. It was the house's only saving grace in Ruth's opinion, and she had expended her best efforts to enhance the room's intrinsic appeal.

One wall was a bank of floor-to-ceiling windows, with French door inserts leading to a stone terrace that fronted the gardens. Her drawings had eliminated the heavy curtains, knocked out the partitioning walls that formed small rooms within the room, opening a large space to light and air.

'What you've done so far is fine, perfect, in fact,' he said. 'But I'll need a full bath in here somewhere, and sleeping quarters. I want this room to be independent of the rest of the house, for I intend to live in it.'

She raised her eyebrows, but nodded without questioning him.

'I isolate myself when I work,' he explained. 'Sometimes for days on end, and if I must live in this house, this room would at least make it tolerable.'

He was silent for a long moment, then he spun away from the windows to face her, his expression superficially bright. 'There! That's it, then. It needs to be finished in six months. Any problem with that?'

'None.'

'Good. I'll stop by once a week to answer any questions that may come up. And now I think we've earned a quiet celebration.' He extended an arm towards the french windows. She shrugged in mild curiosity, then preceded him out to the terrace.

'What's this?' she exclaimed, her face lifting with spontaneous delight.

'I mark the successful closing of any negotiation with some sort of gesture,' he smiled. 'There are too few causes for celebration in this world, so I take full advantage of every one.'

A small, wrought iron table was spread with white linen, and boasted two settings of the most delicate china Ruth had ever seen. The contrast of crystal goblets and silver serving pieces against the backdrop of a sprawling, untended garden was elegant in itself.

She clapped her hands together with undisguised delight. 'How wonderful! Where on earth did you find lilacs at this time of year? It's much too early.'

'They bloom earlier in the South,' he answered, glancing at the heady bouquet in the table's centre. 'Normally I don't indulge in such petty extravagance, but I've always liked lilacs.'

Ruth wondered what memory the humble flower evoked, then lost the thought immediately when he offered her a chair. There was something preposterously luxurious about being seated at such an opulent table in jeans and a sweater. It accentuated the elegance, rather than diminishing it, and she opened all her senses to the pleasure of the moment.

He opened a waiting bottle of champagne with practised ease and filled the two hollow-stemmed crystal goblets. Then with a humorous flourish, he removed the silver domes from side dishes before taking his seat. Enormous fresh strawberries and exquisitely carved melon balls perched on mounds of coloured ices, and Ruth realised for the first time the simple pleasures that wealth could buy.

'I feel positively decadent,' she confided happily. 'Strawberries and lilacs in April, and champagne in the morning. How wonderfully lucky you are to be rich.'

His smile was almost bitter as their glasses touched in a musical ring.

Morning sun bathed the terrace in a warm, golden glow that found Ruth's mass of red hair and danced there in moving points of light. The effects of two glasses of champagne at this early hour showed in the pink flush of her cheeks and over-bright green eyes.

'I haven't had so much fun in years,' she sighed happily. 'I'm going to negotiate many, many deals in my lifetime, so I can celebrate them all like this.'

'Then I wish you great prosperity,' he toasted her with mild amusement. 'You're going to need it if you do this often.'

'You know,' she said thoughtfully, twirling the stem of her glass between two fingers, 'you have a wonderful eye for design. It's not a common trait. So why did you buy this ghastly house?'

She glanced up and saw a muscle tighten in his cheek before he made his reply. 'It was an obligation,' he said shortly, and she chastised herself silently for shattering the festive mood with a thoughtless question.

He refilled their glasses against her vehement, head-shaking protest. 'Champagne doesn't keep,' he said simply. 'One is honour-bound to finish a bottle once it's been opened, especially a vintage as fine as this one.'

She shrugged and raised her glass to her lips, wondering why the bubbly froth didn't seem to affect him at all, when it was making her so very warm.

'You obviously think this house is ill-suited to me,' he continued casually. 'What kind of a house do you see me in?'

She narrowed her eyes dramatically and studied him with affected deep thought, pressing her lips together, then laughing out loud when she found they felt thicker than usual, and slightly numb.

She became immediately solemn, speaking slowly and distinctly, enunciating each word. 'I'm very sorry,' she said carefully, forcing her lips to form the words, blushing with embarrassment. 'I'm not used to champagne—certainly not in the morning. It seems to be affecting my sense of decorum, and my lips.'

'Really?'

'Oh yes. But to answer your question,' she drawled, 'I think a tall house.'

'A tall house?' He raised his brows.

'That's not right,' she frowned. 'I didn't mean tall. I meant ... open. High ceilings, lots of window, lots of space. With a vision ... no, I mean a view. A spectacular view, from a high, high hill.'

'In the back woods somewhere?' he prodded, obviously enjoying her struggle with speech.

'No, no. In the open. Everything open. Light and space. That's you. This is too dark, this awful place.' She waved an arm wildly towards the house. 'And you're already dark, you see. You need light.'

'The mirror contradicts you, Miss Lyons. I'm really quite fair.'

She gave him a foolish smile and closed one eye. 'Not inside, you're not. Inside, you're very, very dark.'

His eyes were perfectly clear and steady as he stared at her. It was her vision that made them appear slightly out of focus.

'Oh my,' she sighed distractedly. 'I'm afraid I have to go home now. I suspect I'm making an absolute fool of myself.'

'I'd be very irresponsible indeed if I allowed you to drive home now, Miss Lyons.' He lifted a sterling coffee pot from the serving cart and filled a delicate china cup before passing it to her. 'Here. Drink up.'

She blew air out through her lips and closed her eyes. 'Ruth,' she said firmly. 'My name is Ruth.'

'As in whither-thou-goest-Ruth?' he asked, smiling tolerantly.

'That's it exactly.' She flashed a lopsided grin. 'That's me.'

'All right, Ruth. Since we're eliminating the formalities, you'll have to call me something other than Mr Hampton. Would you prefer Jonathan, or Tray? Most people call me Tray—an aberration of the French, for third. Pick your pleasure.'

She leaned back in her chair and tipped her head, looking down her nose at him in an attempt to bring him into focus. 'I'd call you spectacular,' she said seriously, with only a slight slur.

'You're going to hate yourself later for that one,' he smiled.

'I know,' she said happily.

He pushed a basket of croissants towards her and stood. 'Grab a couple of those,' he commanded. 'You can eat in the car.'

She frowned, struggling in the fog of her thoughts to find the right words. 'You go,' she said finally. 'I'll sit just a bit before I drive home. Is that all right?'

'No, it isn't,' he replied firmly, pulling out her chair. 'You're coming with me. I'll bring you back to your car later, when you can find the pedals. Besides, there's something I'd like you to see.'

'Are we doing the old whither-thou-goest number?' she giggled.

'Exactly.'

Although she was not aware of the time, it was fully an hour later when the jolting of his small foreign car brought her sharply awake. She straightened in the bucket seat, sleep gone instantly, and peered out at the rough track they were climbing through a thick wood. 'Where on earth are we?' she asked, wincing as the car bounced out of a particularly deep pothole.

'Good morning again,' he smiled, glancing at her briefly before returning his attention to the twisting road. 'Looks like sleep did you a world of good.'

'I can just imagine,' she said ruefully, pushing the disorder of her hair away from her face, wishing for a mirror, then immediately thinking it was probably just as well she didn't have one. A vague memory of her light-headedness of an hour before flitted across her mind, and she grimaced in embarrassment.

At that moment the car broke from the shadows of the last tree line and emerged on to a small, flat meadow that perched so high above the valley below, it gave the illusion of being suspended in mid-air. Ruth caught her breath as the car rolled to a jerky halt, her gaze fixed on that point where the meadow's edge seemed to merge with the sky. She left the car without a word, and as she walked closer to the precipice upon which the small clearing sat, she could begin to see the undulation of golden fields far below as they rolled towards the distant hills. She stopped a foot from the edge and looked out over a world softened by distance. The view was hazy and a little unreal, bringing the place where she stood into sharper focus, as if it were the only place that really existed.

Hampton watched her in silence from the car, studying the lines her body made against the background of the sky. She stood motionless for a long time, with her shoulders thrown back and her head lifted, and there was something challenging about the posture.

'This is it,' she said quietly when she felt his presence move beside her, keeping her eyes focused front. She knew instinctively that this place was uniquely his, and that by bringing her here, he had spoken eloquently of a bond between them that he felt as keenly as she did. She felt an innate sense of belonging, that this place was as much hers as it was his; and thought that if she could stand here like this, with Tray Hampton beside her, she could be happy for the rest of her life.

She felt his eyes on her face, but kept hers purposefully averted, understanding that this was a moment to be prolonged and cherished; one she would pull out of memory later whenever she needed it. The sweep of his gaze was like a physical touch as his eyes roamed the length of her body, then returned to her face. From another man, the inspection would have been insolent, and insulting, but from him, it was the simple act of taking possession, and she never questioned his right to do that. In a strange, inexplicable way, in that moment she belonged to him, and it seemed only right that they both acknowledge it.

'Look at me,' he commanded, and it was yesterday all over again, with a disembodied voice directing her; a voice she would obey without question no matter what it asked.

She turned slowly to face him, and felt the wind lift her hair away from her brow. His eyes bored into hers with a knowledge so complete she felt naked before him. When the wind touched her face again, she shivered, as if it had been his hand tracing a lover's caress across her cheek; his will that directed the wind to touch her for him.

His gaze dropped intentionally to the full lips slightly parted in expectation, and she watched his own mouth tighten into a grim line of denial. Remarkably, unbelievably, his eyes flashed with anger directed towards her, and without seeing them, she knew his fists were clenched at his sides as he fought against the desire to touch her.

There was no reason for his hesitation; no reason for the quivering tension that stretched every muscle in his body as tight as a bowstring; no reason for the anguished fury she saw in the sharp lines of his face. She had known him for weeks, and this moment was simply the inevitable consummation of the emotion that had first rocked her when she saw his handwriting for the very first time. That they were here together, on this magic mountain that belonged to them as surely as if it had been created for this single moment, was only right, and there was only one celebration worthy of this milestone in her life.

She looked directly into his eyes, so he would know she was fully conscious of what she was doing, and reached out to lay her hand on the side of his face. He flinched from her touch, but remained rooted to the spot his body occupied, closing his eyes against what he could read in hers.

'This had to happen,' she whispered, never thinking for a moment that he would not understand the significance of the force that was moving them both; never considering that this would be anything but the momentous beginning of times they were destined to share.

His eyes opened slowly, and travelled the length of her face, down to the visible pulse in her throat that quickened when his gaze touched it. Her chin lifted slightly, almost imperceptibly, and she moistened her parted lips with the tip of her tongue in an unconscious invitation.

There was nothing tender in the sudden grasp of his hands on her shoulders, nor was there gentleness in the violent eyes that sought hers, demanding that she acknowledge this was her desire as well, and that she had brought them to this. She blinked once in silent, willing admission, and felt herself jerked roughly against the unyielding wall of his chest. Hot hands pushed beneath her sweater and splayed open against her back, not in caress or even in exploration, but in a simple, desperate attempt to hold her motionless against him. She felt anger in his hands, saw it in his eyes, and wondered at it; wondered too, why he denied her the touch of his lips, as if kissing would be too personal. She understood suddenly that this was what he wanted; that for some reason beyond her comprehension, he was denying the spiritual need that had prompted their mutual arousal; trying to pretend that this was a physical attraction and nothing more; that he could use her as he would a prostitute. For some reason the realisation made her smile; a slow, lazy, confident smile. Perhaps it was because the feeling of destiny was so strong within her, that even his open denial could not shake it.

When he saw her lips lift, his body shuddered, loosening, and his eyes softened, acknowledging what she had known all along. He released her then, bringing his hands up to thread through her hair, cradling her head while he used his lips sensuously against her chin, her eyelids, her cheeks, pausing at her mouth to pull at her lips, tasting with his tongue. She felt her legs give way and sank to her knees in the dried grass, not at all surprised that he should follow her down, pressed against her, his body merely an extension of hers.

His breath broke against her neck in hot, frantic gasps that echoed her own, and she let her head fall back on her neck as his hands slid down to her hips, pulling them forward.

He pushed himself away long enough to search her face and breathe, 'Here? Now?'

She nodded once, her eyes open and staring, will and thought receding before the throbbing pressure that clamoured for release. He lowered her gently on to her back and remained kneeling next to her, as he would before an altar, his eyes pinning her to the ground, his face moving down towards hers with tortuous slowness. She whimpered into his mouth when it finally covered hers, and arched her back to meet the fiery hand that slipped beneath the front of her sweater, moving slowly upward to cup a bare breast, then down to press insistently against the tightened muscles of her stomach. She was helpless to contain the small cry of pleasure that escaped her throat at that moment, but she would berate herself later for that weakness, for that was what had stopped him. He lifted his body away quickly and stared down at her for a long time, his eyes clouding with a sadness she didn't understand, a crease marring the broad span of his forehead.

A cloud passed over the feeble warmth of the sun, casting a shadow over his face, and suddenly Ruth trembled with a chill that began outside and worked its way in. She sat up shakily, wrapping her arms around her knees, and searched his face. Everything had been right, so absolutely, perfectly right; and then something had gone wrong.

'What is it?' she asked with a trembling voice.

He sat back on his heels, bracing his hands on his thighs, his body rigid with tension. Then his head dropped and his body sagged simultaneously, and a swatch of light hair fell over his forehead and caught the sun. 'I am nothing,' he muttered with self-loathing, 'if not an honourable man.'

She shivered involuntarily, not understanding the words, but knowing that the part of him that denied that bond between them had won, and in so doing, had somehow defeated them both.

It had been a special moment; one of those elusive snatches of life that appear suddenly, out of nowhere; so fleeting and so fragile that only the quick and the sure can capture them before they vanish. But he had turned from it voluntarily, and stolen the moment from both of them.

She stared at his bowed head, wishing it could be recaptured, wishing he had not shattered the magic. 'I don't understand,' she said levelly, controlling the tremor in her voice.

When he raised his eyes she knew she was seeing a Tray Hampton few people, if any, ever saw. His face was open, totally vulnerable; open to regret and frustration, and any wound she cared to inflict.

'Do you offer yourself so easily to any man?' he asked, and because there was no accusation in his tone, no contempt, but merely an attempt to fill the silence, she did not take offence.

'You know I don't,' she replied, and because she had assumed, correctly, that he would know this, he laughed.

'We've barely met, yet you seem to think I know everything about you. Maybe you're giving me too much credit.'

'No,' she whispered. 'You know me, and I know you. I've known you all my life; I just wasn't sure you existed. Laugh if you like, pretend you didn't feel it, too, if that suits your purpose; but I know better.'

His eyes flickered with a remnant of the cynicism she suspected was an integral part of his character. 'Destiny, you mean? Mr and Mrs Right recognising each other from the start? Don't tell me you believe in that nonsense.' His words were mocking, but his tone was almost a plea.

'I didn't,' she said simply, refusing to elaborate.

'But now you do,' he finished for her, turning his head away. 'How embarrassing it would be for you to learn you had made an admission like that to a man who sought only physical satisfaction. Did you ever think of that? That maybe I try to seduce every beautiful woman I meet?'

Her face crumpled in instantaneous despair, for in truth, the thought had never occurred to her.

'Don't look like that,' he said quickly, touching her cheek lightly with one finger, then pulling it away. 'For the record, I don't make a habit of . . .'

'. . . making love to every woman you bring up here?'

'I've never brought a woman here before.' As soon as the sentence had left his lips, his face darkened and he glared at her, realising that he had revealed too much.

But the moment was gone, dissipated by discussing it aloud. They sighed almost in unison.

'So both of us have just behaved out of character,' she said flatly.

'Champagne does that,' he said idly, averting his eyes. Then he rose to his feet and walked to the edge of the cliff, and she felt a door closing against her. Suddenly the morning behind them seemed unreal, like the childish imaginings of some pubescent girl, and Ruth felt the crushing weight of reality suspended above her.

'Why did you say you were an honourable man?' she asked, trying to go back.

'Because I am.'

'But why did you say it *then*?'

'Because what we were about to do was dishonourable.'

'For whom?' she demanded. 'And you don't strike me as the chivalrous type, so don't try to tell me you were saving the fair damsel's honour.'

He turned to her with a smile of bitter irony. 'But that's precisely what I was doing. Only in this case, the fair damsel happens to be the woman I've promised to marry.'

Reality fell brutally then, and for the endless seconds while she felt the aching lump grow in her throat, Ruth wondered if she would ever breathe again. The thought that there might be another woman in his life had never surfaced in her mind, and the stricken look on her face showed that all too clearly. With a start, she realised how foolishly single-minded she had been. He could have been married with a dozen children, and she wouldn't have thought to ask. She had been too caught up with what she was certain was her destiny, and his.

The pain on her face nearly destroyed him, not because he had caused it, but because he understood how much she had surrendered to allow it to show. She was proud, as he was; almost unbearably proud. He had known that from the moment he had first seen her, striding away from him down that long, empty hallway, carrying herself with the air of a conquering soldier, rather than that of a woman who had just been fired. And he had known in that moment that this was a woman who could challenge him like no other, and that life was cruelly ironic to bring them together when it was too late.

'I can see from your face that you think it preposterous another woman would have me,' he said gently, trying to make light of the situation, but she said nothing, nor did she make any attempt to conceal her despair.

Ruth was still sitting on the hill. She could feel the earth and the grass beneath her, so she knew it was still there. It just felt like the world had dropped away, leaving her foolishly suspended above it.

She blinked slowly, then looked up with a broadness of vision that took in the man as a whole, rather than any particular part. She saw him with merciless clarity then, as she would see him a thousand times in her mind during the months to come. He was standing with his back to the world that stretched beneath and beyond the hill's edge; a tall, lean figure framed darkly by the blue sky, his legs spread slightly, his arms held away from his body, palms up, as if he were offering himself to her. Yet there was distance between them that he would not dare bridge again, and she felt the wrenching pain of what might have been pulled away from her by the invisible presence of a woman she could not picture.

That he should destroy her life with one small sentence, then continue to speak conversationally as if nothing had happened seemed almost absurd. She thought she heard apology in his voice.

'We're to be married in October,' he was saying. 'In Europe, at her family's home. Then we'll return to Hampton House.'

She nodded mutely, still trying to conjure up an image of a woman Tray Hampton would marry. No matter how hard she tried, she could see only herself.

'So you see, what almost happened between us ... would have been very unfair.'

'To her, or to me?' she asked caustically, then looked up sharply at his reply.

'To you.'

She rose and moved to face him, staring into the fathomless grey eyes. 'If you mean that,' she said hesitantly, 'then what you're doing is more unfair. To us, and to her.' She spoke quickly, debasing herself in a way she could never have imagined herself doing, leaving herself open to humiliation and rejection and contempt. 'Do you want me?' she demanded, holding her arms out in supplication, and when the whispered, agonised 'yes' was torn from his throat, she pounced on it. 'Then your relationship with her is a lie, a pretence; and honouring it is the worst kind of betrayal.' She flung herself into his arms, pulling his head down to claim his lips with her own, thrusting her body against his with a force that nearly sent them tumbling to the ground. She felt the thrill of satisfaction when a shuddering moan left his throat and broke upon her mouth, and for one exultant moment, when she felt the painful throbbing course from her body into his and back again, she thought she had won.

Then his hands closed on her shoulders and he pushed her away, his arms quivering with the tension of holding her from him while his chest rose and fell with each ragged breath.

'Is this what you want?' he demanded between breaths, his voice harsh and accusing. 'To be mistress? Lover? The other woman? Because that's all I can offer, and all you'd ever have. Was I so wrong to think that was less than what you would demand? Because if I was, then take off your clothes and lie down, and we'll get this the hell over with!'

Her body went instantly cold, and her mind froze. She backed away from his onslaught and barely noticed when his hands slipped from her shoulders.

When he spoke again, his voice was more controlled, but decisive and formal. 'I have absolutely no choice,' he said heavily. 'I will be married in October, and there isn't a single thing that will change that.'

She turned away from him then and gathered the forces discarded earlier, retrieving the bright, hard surface of pride she had let slip away. She waited in the car for a very long time, watching him as he stood on the edge of the hill, wondering what thoughts tormented his mind.

There was no conversation during the ride back to the house; no attempt by either of them to disguise the fact that what had happened on the hill had touched and changed them both. Ruth ran over the events again and again in her mind, trying to feel shame, degradation, hate for the man she sat next to; but she felt none of those things, and although she knew there would be distance between them forever, inexplicably, she had never felt closer to anyone in her life.

The bond between them had been acknowledged, even though consummation had been denied, and nothing could ever destroy that. Not his marriage, or hers, if that should ever happen; not distance, nor time. They were part of each other forever, and nothing could change that either. She wondered if she could endure simple friendship with this man, then wondered if she could live without it.

'Will you still do the house?' he asked when he pulled in behind her car.

He knows, too, she thought. He feels it, too, or he wouldn't understand how difficult this project will be now. But I'm strong enough to do it; strong enough to create a home for the man I want and another woman. And I'll see him. If I work here, I'll see him. I'll have that much, at least.

'Of course,' she answered. 'If you'll answer one question. Truthfully.'

'Anything.'

'Why did you take me there?'

He looked at her silently across the few inches of space that separated them in the small compartment, and let his guard drop long enough for her to see everything in his face. He owed her that, at least.

'Because it was right,' he said. 'That's the only reason I have, no matter how feeble it sounds.'

'That's the only reason you need,' she replied meaningfully, staring straight ahead. 'For anything.'

Her statement was a rebuke for not following other instincts on the hill that had been just as right, and sensing that, he offered a token defence.

'I've been engaged for fifteen years,' he said.

She raised her eyebrows in surprise. 'That doesn't sound like you were too anxious to marry this woman,' she countered, suddenly hopeful again.

'There were problems. Problems for Christie. She didn't think I should be burdened with them. Waiting was her idea.'

'And now they're gone?'

'For the most part, yes.'

She thought Christie was a particularly inane name for a grown woman. It sounded fluffy, and insipid. 'You don't want to tell me what the problems were?'

'Another time, perhaps.'

'Sounds like your Christie,' she emphasised the name with disdain, 'is the self-sacrificing type.'

'Very much so.'

'And very unlike me.'

He laughed at that. 'Very. She's also thoughtful, patient, and kind.'

'She sounds like a Golden Retriever I had once.'

'And you sound like a cat I had once,' he said gently, turning in the seat to face her.

He smiled sadly, and the tension eased somewhat, as if the tempest of their relationship had shifted subtly into a lower, less demanding gear.

'I think I like you, you know,' she said suddenly, not knowing what made her say it. 'Apart and aside from the rest, I do like you.'

'I'll value that,' he said sombrely. 'Apart and aside from the rest, I'll value that most of all.'

'Well,' she sighed, leaning back against the seat, rubbing her eyes. 'That's easier. Having it all out in the open, being able to talk about it; that makes it easier. You refuse to be lovers, so we'll be friends. That's all you'll offer, and since I have no pride left at all, I'll take it.'

His expression was troubled and guarded, and she laughed easily when she saw it. 'Don't look so concerned,' she chided him. 'If I can handle it, you certainly should be able to. I can't stand it when people bury things away, pretending they never happened. It happened, and that's that. Accept it and go on from there. Does it embarrass you that I almost succeeded in seducing you?'

'It was not a trivial thing,' he said earnestly, fixing her with his gaze. 'I can't talk about it with that kind of casual disregard.'

'Veneer, my dear,' she smiled condescendingly. 'It's only veneer. Now. When do I meet Mrs Not-So-Right?'

His smile was faint, flashing on and off so fast she wondered if it had been there at all. 'Soon. This house was her choice, not mine, by the way, so she'll want to be here a good part of the time to watch the work progress.'

'How nice,' she said sarcastically, 'I take it she at least liked my designs.'

'Lord, no!' His laugh was hard and brittle. 'She hasn't even seen them yet, but to give you an idea of how she'll react, that foyer design that cost you your job was hers. I learned that last night.'

'What!' Ruth flared, twisting to face him. 'That design was hers?'

'I'm afraid so. She created it, had it drawn up, and sent to each designer submitting a bid. Without my knowledge, by the way.'

Ruth closed her eyes and faced front again, never believing for a moment that any woman who designed such a horror could be either thoughtful, patient, or kind, as he had described her. The foyer revealed a much grimmer picture of its creator; one Ruth found distinctly unpleasant. It frustrated her that this man, this supposedly bright, perceptive genius of business, could not see that too. 'Anyone who liked that foyer will hate my designs,' she said cryptically. 'That should be obvious even to you.'

'Probably.'

'And she'll fight me every step of the way. It's to be her house, after all. You can't expect her to accept something she'll hate without putting up a fight of some sort.'

His face seemed to draw in on itself. 'I promised you no interference from anyone, and my word is good. Agreeing to live in that pile of rubble was my one and only compromise, and Christie knows that. Your designs stand, exactly as they are.'

Ruth frowned at the hostility in his voice, baffled by the resentment he obviously harboured against the woman he was going to marry, wondering what bond could be so strong to justify a marriage even he questioned.

She felt the weight of her body suddenly, and found it difficult to summon the energy required to climb out of the car. She closed the door quietly behind her, then stooped to poke her head back through the window.

'You're marrying the wrong woman,' she said flatly, her green eyes challenging his.

His gaze seemed to draw her closer and closer to his face, until all she was conscious of seeing was his eyes, penetrating her mind, exposing her thoughts; laying her bare.

'I know that,' he said in a near whisper, and although his voice had the ring of finality, his hand reached out to brush a stray wisp of red curl from her brow in a gesture so touching she was powerless to move away from it. His fingers strayed to her lips and lingered there momentarily while his eyes held hers, then, just as her lips parted under the sweetness of his touch, he dropped his hand.

He cleared his throat and settled more deeply into his seat. 'I'll have a copy of the plans dropped at your apartment tonight,' he said stiffly. 'Would eight o'clock be convenient?'

She nodded once, then straightened slowly and watched his car pull away.

CHAPTER THREE

ALL things considered, it would prove to be the most exhausting day of Ruth's life. After the emotional peaks and depths of the morning, she sought solace in a frenzy of activity. She met Sally for lunch, and the younger woman's delighted enthusiasm for her unexpected good fortune helped push back the disappointment of her aborted relationship with Hampton.

'Have you called the agent about the Market Street property?' Sally demanded after the initial congratulatory excitement. 'And how about the plasterers, and the carpenters, and the plumbers, and what are you going to call yourself? His lawyers will need a name, you know. You can't incorporate without one. And how about office furniture? I suppose you could lease some of it, but . . .'

'Sally, Sally,' Ruth laughed, holding her hands up in mock surrender. 'I haven't done anything yet. I came straight here from the house.'

Sally shook her head in the tolerant, almost fond exasperation of a parent dealing with a terribly disorganised child. 'Well,' she sighed, 'there's certainly plenty to be done before the day's out. I'd better get started.'

Ruth's brows tipped in an amused frown. 'Now? You're going to start now?'

'You hired me, didn't you?'

'Well, yes, but your job . . . you'll have to give notice to Harold . . .'

'Oh, to hell with Harold,' she said peevishly, and Ruth barely suppressed a giggle. She would not have thought sweet Sally capable of cursing under any circumstances, but was fast suspecting that she knew very little about this woman. The no-nonsense dynamo of energy sitting across from her barely resembled the quiet, innocuous girl she had known at Westchester.

'I'm going back to the office just long enough to pack my desk and stick my tongue out at Harold,' Sally continued, 'then I'll go straight home and get to work from there.'

'That's going to look lousy on a resumé, Sally,' Ruth pointed out. 'No notice, no references, you know.'

'Do I need a reference from Harold Westchester to work for you?'

'Lord, no, but . . .'

'But nothing. Then I don't need his reference at all, because working for you is the last job I'll need.'

'And what if Hampton House is the first and last contract I get? Then where will you be?'

'No chance,' Sally said with a confident shake of her head. 'In the first place, you'll be famous after this. You'll have more work than you can handle. But even if people don't come running to you, you'll find work somehow. You're one of those people who can't live without it, and as long as you have work, I'll have work.'

Ruth cupped her chin in her hand and looked at Sally with mystified wonder. 'How is it that you know so much about me, Sally, and I know so little about you?'

'You're easy to read,' Sally replied. 'Creative people usually are. They're also notoriously oblivious to things which have nothing to do with their work, which explains why you know nothing about the people around you.'

Ruth blinked at the decidedly accurate summation of her character, promising herself to be more observant in the future.

'Don't look so guilty,' Sally chided her, reading Ruth's expression, as she said she could, very easily indeed. 'Most people aren't worth knowing anyway.'

'You know that's not true, Sally,' she said softly. 'You just made me realise how much I must have missed by being so single-minded about my work.'

'Well, you're not too old to learn,' Sally shrugged, lightening the mood. 'Although you'll need watching. You're a dreadful judge of character. Remember Mr Waverly's son? The one you thought was such a splendid young man?'

'Yes. What about him?'

'His father swore out a warrant for his arrest yesterday. Seems he skipped to Brazil with the best part of the family art collection.'

Ruth's mouth dropped open. 'Billy Waverly? I can't believe it! He was such a . . .'

'. . . nice young man?' Sally finished with a smug smile. 'See what I mean? You need protection from the wolves, boss; and I'm just the girl who can do it. Believe it or not, we're going to make a great team. Now let's get down to business.'

Sally hustled right into a hurried discussion of what had to be accomplished within the next few hours, assigning most of the administrative chores to herself. Ruth listened patiently, answering questions when necessary, making all the proper responses, wondering all the while how she ever would have managed such a day without Sally. There was an instant of revelation when she realised that in one day she had made the second and third friends of her lifetime, and her face lifted with a beautiful smile, which had no place in their conversation, and puzzled Sally. She frowned briefly, then chattered on, undaunted, while Ruth remembered Martin, her first friend, and the only one for a very long time. It seemed fitting that it would take two to replace him.

At five o'clock Ruth literally stumbled into her apartment and collapsed on the nearest chair. Within four hours she had leased the Market Street property, purchased the bare minimum of furnishings and equipment, and drafted a rough schedule of workmen needed for Sally's administration. She had been out of her apartment too much to intercept any calls from Hampton's attorneys, lingering only long enough to take delivery on the promised bank draft; but all in all, the day had been as productive as it had been exhausting.

She closed her eyes and welcomed sleep with a mind at once uncluttered, but where sleep should have come creeping, a picture of Hampton came instead. She saw him as he had been on the hill, facing her, his back to the sky, his posture triumphant as if he had stormed the hill in battle and claimed it for his own. She clamped her eyes more tightly shut and willed the vision away, but already it had planted a seed of emptiness within her, and she rose tiredly from the chair and tried to fill her thoughts with other things.

She showered, dressed carelessly in sweat pants and an oversized shirt, washed her hair and let it drip on her shoulders as it dried into shining, red curls. She rinsed the cup left from morning coffee she had drunk a lifetime ago, then cleaned the small apartment with near-vicious intensity, finding drawers to organise, glass to be polished, and a hundred other things she would never normally think of doing.

By eight o'clock there was nothing left to do; nothing physical to fill the time and deplete her strength and save her from the sad torment of the morning's memories.

She stood forlornly in the small galley kitchen, her shoulders slumped in defeat, her eyes cast down, wishing nothing as fervently as she wished that she had never heard of Hampton House, or of the man who owned it.

The door buzzer startled her out of the self-pitying reverie, and she nearly flew to answer it, remembering that Hampton had promised to have copies of the plans delivered tonight, and that she had alterations to make on them. Nothing would empty her mind as effectively as work, and she flung open the door with a look of bright expectation.

'You!' she exhaled, feeling all the breath leave her body.

'That's an ambiguous greeting,' he smiled, leaning against the doorframe, a large manila envelope dangling from one hand.

'I didn't expect you,' she said stupidly, still surprised that the man standing before her did not wear the dull brown uniform of a messenger.

He drew himself slowly erect and stood silently before her, his eyes sweeping her body with the now-familiar air of possession. She had time to notice that he was dressed formally; that he looked as self-assured and elegant in tie and tails as he had in jeans; that the long lines of his body seemed made for the crisp detail of formal wear, as they did for anything he wore. The old adage about clothes making the man popped ludicrously into her mind, and she dismissed it immediately. In this case, the man made the clothes, whatever they were.

'You look magnificent,' she said without thinking, and watched his face lift into an expression of amused pleasure.

'You're not particularly coy,' he smiled, stepping through the entrance and pulling the door closed behind him. 'Do you always say precisely what you're thinking?'

'I'm afraid so,' she answered, moving aside to accommodate his presence in the tiny foyer, backing into the wall in her haste to be out of his way.

'That will take some getting used to. I've never had a totally honest relationship with anyone in my life.'

He wandered through the small apartment, his eyes busy, taking in every detail, his hands darting out now and then to touch a wall, or a piece of furniture. She followed him like an obedient shadow, her brows furrowed, never thinking to question his right to examine her surroundings as if he had just purchased the apartment and everything in it.

He stopped in the living room and turned to face her. 'You actually live here?' he asked quietly. 'I can't see any evidence of you anywhere in the whole apartment. It looked like one of those models, with no character at all.'

She looked around quickly, dismayed by what she was seeing for the first time through someone else's eyes. Bland, unimaginative furnishings; a glaring lack of personal items that give a home the personality of its owner; even the walls were hospital white and barren. She had lived here for five years and never noticed its emptiness before.

'I rented it furnished,' she said lamely. 'It's just a place to sleep.'

He shook his head in disbelief, dislodging a lock of light hair that fell disarmingly over his forehead. 'Probably the most creative interior designer in the country, and you live in a place like this. Unbelievable. Don't bring any other clients here, Ruth. It's not great advertising. You look tired.'

Then he added such a personal observation fast on the heels of his criticism of her apartment disoriented her slightly.

'I am tired,' she said defensively. 'It's been a busy day.'

'You should have gone to bed right after supper.'

'Maybe I will.'

'Maybe you will?' he repeated. 'You mean you haven't eaten yet? It's past eight o'clock. How about lunch? Did you eat lunch?'

She frowned at his sudden, possessive interest in her eating habits. 'Of course I had lunch,' she shot back, a little irritated. 'I had . . .' She closed her eyes and tried to remember. '. . . a salad, I think.'

He flattened his lips in exasperation and pushed past her towards the kitchen. 'Is there anything edible in this place?' he demanded, opening and closing cupboard doors, rummaging through the refrigerator.

'What are you? My keeper?' she asked indignantly.

'Looks like you need one,' he muttered, then straightened and shook his head. 'I give up. A mouse would starve in this place. Where's the 'phone?'

She listened as he ordered a delivery from some delicatessen she had never heard of; then as he placed one more call, cancelling his plans for the evening.

'Now just what do you think you're doing?' she asked when he had replaced the receiver, her arms crossed in front of her.

'I'm insuring that you're in condition to start work on my house tomorrow,' he replied gruffly, but she heard the caring in his voice, and smiled in response.

'You're taking care of me,' she accused him playfully. 'It's the oldest instinct in the world. A man takes care of his woman.'

He sighed heavily. 'You never give up, do you?'

'Not when I'm right.'

He shook his head in disbelief. 'You're the most aggressive, forward woman alive. You must be. Also shameless,' he added.

For some reason that gave her pause, and she moved to a cupboard over the refrigerator without making a response.

'Wine?' he noted with surprise as she pulled down a bottle and two glasses. 'You actually keep wine on hand? I didn't think you were that civilised.'

'I'm not. Martin kept my cupboard pretty well-stocked. He claimed a home without wine was habitation "fit only for beasts", or something like that.'

'I hate to admit this, but I think I would have liked Martin.'

She set the glasses carefully on the small dinette table and looked at him steadily. 'You would have loved Martin. You wouldn't have been able to help yourself.'

He studied her intently for a moment. 'You did, didn't you?'

'Yes.'

'And he loved you?'

'Yes.'

He nodded absently, then relieved her of the corkscrew and bottle. 'Good Lord,' he said, frowning, noticing the label for the first time. 'Do you realise what this is?'

'It's wine, of course,' she answered impatiently. 'Red, I think.'

He laughed uproariously. 'You have a remarkable gift for understatement! I know of no one else who would describe Chateau Lafite's '59 claret as merely "red wine"! Do you have any idea of the value of this bottle? And you were going to have it with deli!'

She shrugged nonchalantly. 'It's all I have here. Two dozen bottles of that stuff.'

'Two dozen?'

'About that. There may be more in the vault. I haven't checked.' She followed his puzzled expression and explained. 'Martin left his wine cellar to me. He arranged to have it stored by one of the local importers. I have a list here somewhere.'

'Find it,' he ordered brusquely.

She remembered then that she had put the list in her safety deposit box, and told him so; a revelation he greeted with a frustrated moan. 'I'll make a copy next time I go to the bank,' she mollified him.

By the time he had answered the door, accepted the boxes of food and paid the delivery boy, she had the wine opened.

'Oh no,' he moaned, watching the precious fluid splash into the inexpensive wine glasses. 'You should have saved that.'

'For what? They made it to drink, didn't they?'

He released a sigh so filled with despair it was comical, and she laughed as she raised her glass.

'To friendship,' she said simply, and their thick glasses touched with an unmusical click.

He had two glasses of wine, savouring every sip; she had one; then they attacked the mountains of crusty rolls, spicy meats and cheeses he had ordered. Midway into the meal, he stood long enough to remove his jacket and strip off his tie.

'Where were you going?' she asked him.

'Just to the theatre, then to dinner. Nothing important.'

'Business?'

'Not exactly.'

'Your fiancée?'

'No,' he said flatly. 'She's not due back from Europe until Thursday.'

She wondered if there were yet other women he saw socially, then almost hoped there were, just for the satisfaction of knowing he had cancelled an evening with one of them to spend it with her.

He moved his arm to reach for another roll, and she saw his shirt cuff brush dangerously close to a pat of hot mustard.

'Just a minute,' she ordered, rising from her chair and moving to where his sat turned sideways from the table. She stepped between his knees, lifted one of his wrists, and released the catch on a small, exquisite gold and diamond cufflink. She removed it from the cuff, set it carefully on the table, then proceeded to roll the cuff up on his forearm. Her hair fell over her face as she bent her head to the task, creating a shimmering, living veil that quivered with the motions of her hands.

She shifted her gaze slightly when her fingers brushed against his bare skin, and saw that his eyes were riveted to hers, mere inches away. She stopped breathing then, and knew that he had too.

Sinking slowly to her knees before his chair was not a

conscious gesture of supplication, for she was incapable of such a thing. It was simply that his gaze affected her balance, and she felt safer, more secure, kneeling on the floor while she finished a task that seemed suddenly critical, requiring her complete concentration.

She raised her eyes to meet his once again, extending her hand palm up for his other wrist. He offered it wordlessly, his eyes darkening, and from the outer edge of her vision she saw the long muscles in his thighs tighten beneath the smooth fabric that covered them.

A picture she had seen a dozen times during her childhood flashed into her mind; a picture of a woman kneeling at a man's feet, offering his slippers. She had always hated that painting, hated the woman in it, for subjugating herself so shamelessly to a man. And yet at that moment, she felt a kinship with that painted, one-dimensional woman she would have been unable to articulate; a deep and complete understanding that the physical act of kneeling can never debase anyone, unless they kneel spiritually as well. As she knelt before Tray Hampton now, astounding him with the extent and the nature of her capacity to give, she was offering only what she was willing to let him have, not whatever he was capable of taking, and she had never felt such nobility of purpose.

Remarkably, he understood this, and was humbled by it.

Her fingers moved nimbly and without hesitation, rolling up the second cuff, then sliding up to cross his chest and rest at his throat. She felt the strong pulse there beneath her fingers; felt the deeper, more distant throb of his heart further below. With her hands splayed across his chest, she felt it rise quickly in two sharp breaths, and her body inclined slightly forward in unbidden response until one breast brushed against his knee. The nipple blossomed instantly beneath the thin fabric of her shirt, thrusting forward into an almost painful point of increased sensitivity. She saw his eyes

drop to the deep v-neck that opened on a cleavage of
breasts taut and swollen and demanding, and caught
her own breath when his head rolled back slightly and
his lips parted. He was almost panting by the time she
had removed the first three studs from his shirt, and she
rose on shaky legs, her breasts pulsing inches from his
face, her stomach hot and churning. His skin was tightly
drawn across the planes of his cheeks, emphasising the
intensity of grey eyes gone nearly black, then she felt
the screaming tension radiating from his body snap
with an almost audible release. He jerked her to him
then, burying his head in the valley between her breasts,
pushing her shirt aside and closing his lips around the
tightened, responsive peak of one mound. She sagged
against him with a small cry, her head thrown back,
then felt the chill of air against her exposed breast as he
pushed her abruptly from him.

She looked down in confusion, watched him breathe
rapidly through his mouth with his eyes pressed tightly
shut, then saw the stiffness of control find its way back
into his face as his eyes fluttered open.

'That's a very tempting offering,' he said hoarsely,
nodding towards her breasts, 'but it's carrying
friendship a little too far, don't you think?'

She went suddenly cold, humiliated only because he
was stronger than she was, knowing that she could
never have reached this point of arousal and turned
away, as he had.

'Your willpower is remarkable,' she said bitterly,
looking down at the strain on his face, satisfying herself
that at least the effort had cost him. 'But it's getting
harder, isn't it?'

'You don't have to look so smug. I never thought it
would be easy.' He pushed further away gently, then
snugged his chair under the table and returned his
attention to the food.

She returned to her chair and picked at the food on
her plate, watching him with undisguised interest.

'What if I told you that being your mistress would be enough?' she asked suddenly, and he glanced up with a quick, harsh look of reprimand.

'You'd be lying to yourself, and it wouldn't last. You'd hate me soon enough, and then we wouldn't have friendship either.'

He put his food down, wiped his hands carefully on a napkin, then reached across the table to pull her hands towards him. He spoke with a deep, chilling earnestness, looking directly into her eyes. 'Yesterday I would have laughed at any man who said the things I'm about to say to you. Even now, I can barely believe them myself.' He spoke quickly, letting the words run together, afraid to pause for fear he would never start again. 'I knew what you were, Ruth, the first moment I saw you, although I fought against it as long as I could.' He broke off to laugh in cold self-derision. 'That's rich, isn't it? As long as I could stand it turned out to be less than one day. It was like recognising someone you had only seen in paintings, or photographs; someone you always hoped existed, but never really believed in. That was what it was like, seeing you for the first time. And I knew you were that person, before you spoke a single word. There you were, standing alone in that empty hallway, and I knew in that instant that for the rest of my life, you would be a part of me. That's preposterous, isn't it? Fairytale stuff.'

Ruth felt the tears hammering for exit behind her eyes, for he was telling her her own feelings, and she felt at once as if she were one person split into two parts; that this man was not a separate individual, but only that part of her she had been missing for so long.

'I have to have you in my life, Ruth, can you understand that? And if taking you as a lover means losing you later, which it would, then it's a risk I'll never take. You're too important.'

She nodded, understanding a little then, because she felt the same way. It was why she could still work on his house, knowing he would live there with another woman, because at least it would keep her close to him. He would still be a part of her life. But she didn't understand the most important part, and lack of understanding made her angry.

She let the tear fall as she jerked her hands away from his, one gesture contradicting the other. 'So we both suffer,' she complained bitterly, 'and your fiancée, too. She will suffer most of all, just because you refuse to break a promise you made fifteen years ago. Hampton, that's just plain stupid, and cruel!'

He looked down at his open palms, strangely cold without hers touching them, then curled them into white fists. Then he forced his fingers to relax and open, sighed deeply, and finished his wine. 'Do you have anything stronger?' he asked. 'I'd hate to open another bottle of this.'

She went wordlessly to the cupboard, retrieved a bottle of Martin's twenty-year-old brandy, and filled a water glass to the top. He downed a full third of it before setting the glass carefully on the table in front of him.

'Fifteen years ago I was an irresponsible twenty-year-old,' he began, 'drunk on champagne, and youth, and power, and having the time of my life at Christie's coming out party. She was young, and innocent, and achingly lovely, and my fondest, drunken intention was to take her away somewhere that night and seduce her. Instead of the motel I had in mind, we ended up wrapped around a telephone pole, Christie's face through the windshield, the dashboard crushing her legs.'

He swallowed deeply of the brandy, and a fine sheen of perspiration broke out on his forehead. 'In one reckless, drunken moment, I had managed to transform the state's most desirable, eligible debutante into a hopeless, hideous cripple, with slim chance of survival, let alone prospects for the bright future that had been hers moments before.'

Ruth felt her face tighten, aching for the pain of memory she saw twisting his features. 'Were you hurt?' she whispered.

'Of course not!' he laughed coldly. 'I was too drunk, and too damnably lucky. But Christie was; irreparably. Her many suitors disappeared one by one; it took only one look at what remained in that hospital bed, you see. And when it became miraculously apparent that she would live to suffer what I had done to her, I knew her life was my responsibility. I proposed while she still had tubes running in and out of her body.'

'And she accepted?' Ruth asked, unbelieving. 'I would have thought . . .'

'. . . that she would hate the sight of me? That was the worst part; the particularly nasty cross I will bear until the day I die. She never condemned me once; never blamed me; never hated me. She defended me constantly against the accusations of her parents, and her brother, and others who held me accountable, as I deserved. The guilt would have been easier to bear if she had only hated me, but she never did. She was in physical agony for years, enduring countless surgeries to reconstruct her face; pleading with me constantly to get on with my life, to leave her behind, to find another woman. When she finally accepted the fact that I would not relent, that I intended to marry her and take care of her for the rest of our lives, she made only one request—that we wait until her surgery schedule was complete. She was adamant about that. In her words, she said she would not have her husband "tied to a monster".'

'Oh, my God,' Ruth murmured, absorbing the horror; the vacant, empty years; touched by reluctant respect for a woman she wanted desperately to hate.

'So!' he snapped, banging the table with the flat of his hand, making Ruth jump. 'After forty operations, the last of which took place five months ago, she set the date. Six months from now. In Switzerland, where her family moved to be close to the plastic surgeon who put her back together.'

Ruth didn't know how to ask the question that came immediately to mind. 'What does she . . .' she began lamely, and he smiled with a strange bitterness.

'. . . look like? Exactly as she did then. It's frightening, really. Every time I look at her it's like going back to that night, living it all over again. She's beautiful, by anyone's standards; as breathtaking as she was fifteen years ago. More so, in a way, because she seems so much at peace. Content, I guess. It radiates from her.' He shrugged, unable to find the proper words to describe it. 'But she's still in a wheelchair, and she always will be. Apparently a spinal nerve was crushed, and there was nothing the surgeons could do about that.'

He poured himself another measure of brandy, and Ruth watched as he tossed it back, her body and her mind numb. 'Do you love her?' she asked hesitantly, almost afraid to hear the answer.

One side of his mouth twisted in an unpleasant attempt at a smile. 'Let's just say I'm devoted to her. There is nothing I would not do to spare her hurt of any kind. I will be as much as I can be for her, and since she seems to love me . . .' He lifted broad shoulders in a disjointed shrug, and Ruth saw from the slow, languorous blinks that the enormous quantity of liquor he had consumed was at last taking effect. 'That's astounding, isn't it?' he mumbled, almost to himself. 'That she could love a man who did that to her?'

Ruth nodded sadly, thinking that it was indeed astounding; almost unbelievable. She fought back the waves of self-pity. She should be feeling sorry for that poor woman, she admonished herself silently; and for this man, who carried the awful burden of such guilt, forced to let it shape his life. And yet she could not stop mourning for herself; understanding at last, knowing she would never have completely the man she loved.

Now she, too, felt bound by the honour of the word he had given fifteen years ago; restricted by the sacred trust he had taken upon himself. Never again could she consciously ask him to violate that trust.

She screwed her eyes shut in frustration, wishing he had not told her.

Whether it was the liquor, or the emotional depletion following his story, Hampton did not resist her suggestion that he spend the night, perhaps because he understood there was no risk now in such a situation.

Ruth tossed restlessly in her bed after seeing him slip into the untroubled sleep of exhaustion on the couch, and returned to the living room several times during the night, just to look at him. Once she reached out and smoothed the unruly light strands of his hair away from his brow, letting her fingers linger on the smooth heat of his forehead. Tenderness welled within her until she thought her body would overflow with it. He slept on, his face younger by years in repose, and strangely innocent.

She fell into fitful slumber near dawn, and when she awoke an hour later, he was gone.

CHAPTER FOUR

FOR over a week the busy, discordant sounds of hammers and saws and drills and lathes had shattered the still, country air around Hampton House. It was a wild, frantic orchestration of noise that filled the mind and dulled the senses, and as long as Ruth could hear it, she could forget about Hampton for minutes at a time.

'I don't know how you stand all this racket!' Sally had complained the one time she visited the site.

'I love it,' Ruth had answered, so quietly that Sally had been forced to tip her head close to Ruth's mouth to hear the words.

'You could go deaf out here!' Sally had shouted. 'You can't even hear yourself think!'

Ruth had smiled a sombre little smile, and nodded.

'Well if anyone tells you you're not crazy, don't believe them!'

But there was small chance of that. If anyone had recognised the trim, grimy figure in coveralls and duckbill hard hat as a woman at all, they wouldn't have credited her with common sense, let alone sanity.

She was at the site from dawn to dusk, hustling from one room to another, supervising three crews of burly, work-hardened men whose reluctance to take orders from a petite, exacting woman had been initially obvious. Two of them had taken one look at her on the first day, thrown their hats on the ground in disgust, and walked off the job. The remaining men had been sullen at first, and intentionally disagreeable, but after a few days on the job, most seemed to have forgotten that she was a woman at all.

She didn't act like a woman, for one thing, at least not the way these men expected a woman to act. All of their chauvinist instincts, and all of their chivalrous ones as well, flew in the face of the asexual person who represented herself as The Boss, and nothing more. There was nothing feminine or masculine about Ruth Lyons when she worked, and because she presented neither image, there was no threat in her authority. Besides, if you looked her straight in the eye when she talked to you, ignoring the rest of her face and her body, you saw only the confidence and the purpose that drove her, and could forget for minutes at a time that she was even a person at all. It was the force of her mind that the men obeyed, and gradually came to respect.

Ruth was dimly aware of this peculiar ability of hers to bypass the sexual role struggles so prevalent in a society where women were just beginning to alter their stations. But it never occurred to her that she should be a soldier in that great, creeping army of liberation; or that she strolled easily across bridges women had been storming noisily for years. She was simply one more person in a world filled with people, doing a job, expecting nothing more than to be judged by her abilities, as she judged others.

It was a naïve, simplistic philosophy, and it crumbled easily in social situations where men and women still draw hard, black lines of demarcation defining their separate roles. But here, on the job, where walls fell or stood only on the basis of whether the exacting laws of science were applied, honesty worked. It was the only thing that did.

It amused her in a bitter sort of way that these macho, physical men could accept her for what she was, while their more educated, pseudo-intellectual brothers could not. They filled their time and emptied their heads with hour upon tedious hour of discussing whether or not women would ever be truly accepted as people apart from their sex. But to these supposedly die-hard chauvinist, blue-collar workers, she was simply a person, and incidentally, their boss; while in every drawing room she had ever entered, she was first, foremost, and forever, a woman.

After a full week as a person she wondered if she could ever go back to being just a woman again. She had met two men in her life that made her feel like both. One was dead, and one was unattainable. She didn't know what the odds were against ever meeting another, but she suspected sadly that they were very slim indeed.

Martin had been friend, confidant, and a creative equal; yet beneath all that there had always been an underlying tenderness; that solicitous caring that marks the father-daughter relationship so clearly. At times she had been his equal, and at times she had been the woeful daughter seeking comfort; and he had very nearly made her whole, by giving her the freedom to be both.

There was a lingering sense of betrayal that he had died without a word of farewell; without a word to mark the affection between them; on one of those rare evenings they had not spent together. 'You need more time to yourself, Ruth,' he had scolded her. 'Go out, meet people your own age, fall in love, make a life for yourself. You're wasting your youth on a tired old man.' Those had been his last words to her; words that sent her away. She had questioned his real feelings for her ever since. That doubt isolated her, and made her reluctant to ever give her heart again.

And then had come Hampton, shooting into her life like a fireball, burning away doubt and rational thought, igniting a desire she never knew she possessed. It destroyed her resolve to remain solitary, and consumed her with a bright, white heat that left her as open and vulnerable as a new wound. It forced her to face some shocking truths about herself, the most disturbing being that this man made her feel like a woman first, and a person second. And that she wanted that; needed it; clung to it like a drowning man clings to a piece of flotsam that appears magically next to him in a thousand square miles of empty sea. This is the way it should be, she realised. She would be person first to every other man in the world, Martin included; but to Hampton, she was a woman. Anything else was second-best.

She had always offered herself proudly, as if her love were some shining gift, bright and clean, beyond value, that could not possibly be refused. And yet they all left the gift behind: first her mother, then Martin, and now Hampton. This was the fall her mother had always talked about; the terrible, soul-wrenching tumble from the heights that pride occupied. She wondered if she would ever recover.

Hampton appeared at the site twice during that first week, and though Ruth tried to remain unmoved, tried to shield herself with the feeble cushion of timeworn pride, she failed miserably. Her heart leaped to her throat each time his tall, lean figure appeared unexpectedly in the haze of cement dust the workmen's tools raised. She could feel her face transform as she watched him move through the clutter with a strange, aloof elegance; and wondered that the glow she felt didn't shine from her face with a visible aura. Even if no one else could see it, surely he could. And if he looked closely enough, perhaps he could also see the empty, formless pain that resided beneath the glow. The two emotions waged constant war in his presence: exultation that he existed; pain that he could never be hers.

Their conversations had been light and unstrained, and she felt the deep bond of friendship strengthening all out of proportion to the time they spent together. But there was also a tense undercurrent of other, deeper emotions, struggling to surface. Ruth thought any fool who cared to look would have been able to see the truth.

'Any of the men giving you trouble?' he asked when he saw her fielding questions from a brute twice her breadth and height.

'Of course not,' she answered in the light, casual tone she forced whenever they talked. She could not help herself. She could not stop trying to force verbal affirmation of the feelings they shared. She disguised her intent with a playful tease. 'But if they do, will you strike them down with your white sword?'

He let his eyes roam pointedly over her dusty coveralls and distinctly unfeminine boots. 'You look like you're perfectly capable of taking care of yourself,' he smiled, then added, 'By the way, the attorneys tell me you're an official corporation now. Where did you get the name "Summit Design"?'

'From where it all began,' she answered softly.

His eyes narrowed slightly and he nodded. 'The hill. I thought so.' He tore his eyes from hers and looked away. 'I'm going to call it that, if you don't mind. The Summit.'

'You're naming the hill?'

'I'm naming the house that will be built on the hill.' He turned back towards her with a smile in his eyes. 'I need an interior designer to work with the architect. Interested?'

She took a deep breath and exhaled shakily, opening her mouth to speak, but no words would come.

The smile spread from his eyes to his mouth. 'I thought you might be. I'll pick you up at your apartment Saturday noon. We're lunching with the architect. Between the two of you, you should be able to come up with a house worthy of the name.'

She woke Saturday morning with a dull, nervous burning in the pit of her stomach. She had never collaborated with an architect before. Her specialty had always been the renovation of existing houses, and she wasn't sure she was temperamentally suited to sharing and co-ordinating ideas with anyone else. And this house was so important. It would be the work of her life; the project for which everything else she had done merely prepared her. It would be her house, hers and Hampton's; and even though she knew they would never live there together, she would design the interior for that purpose. If the architect would let her.

She mumbled to herself as she showered and washed her hair, picturing a stodgy, conservative, stuffy old man who wore three-piece suits to bed and hadn't seen a building site in years.

'I might as well dress to please the old bozo,' she muttered, pulling a cream linen suit from the long rack of business clothes that had lately taken a back seat to jeans.

She was ready by eleven o'clock, and spent the next hour pacing her small apartment with the frustration of a caged animal. She jumped when the door buzzer sounded, then rushed to answer it, flinging the door open impatiently.

Hampton's eyes caught hers with an intensity that made her words of greeting stick in her throat, and she stood silently under his gaze, helpless to move or to speak.

If ever in the last week she had wondered if his desire for her still lived, she found the answer now in his eyes. They narrowed as they travelled down the length of the straight, slim skirt, then moved up again to touch that point where the suit's jacket opened to show the lacy camisole underneath. His gaze took in the flush of her cheeks, the shimmering halo of golden red framing her face, the brilliant flash of green eyes bright with suppressed excitement. Then without saying a word, without even giving the impression of motion, he slipped inside the door, closed it quickly behind him, unbuttoned her jacket and slid it from her shoulders.

'My God, you're beautiful,' he murmured while his hands moved up and down her bare arms.

The jacket fell unnoticed to the floor while she trembled there before him, her eyes closing languorously, her lips parted, waiting without question for whatever he cared to do. She shuddered when his hands brushed over the twin mounds rising beneath the thin camisole, listening to the music of his breathing as hot puffs of air burst against her neck. His fingers pushed deeply into the flesh of her shoulders as his lips touched that line where fabric met skin on her breast; then she heard his sigh of resignation, and opened her eyes to find his focused on some distant point over her left shoulder.

'We'll be late,' he said perfunctorily, pushing her away.

She willed his eyes to meet hers while she held her breath, and failing in that, bent to retrieve her jacket from the floor.

'I apologise,' he said stiffly as she rearranged her clothes. 'That wasn't fair to either of us. I'm just making it more difficult.'

There was nothing to say to that, so she followed him out of the door in silence, regaining emotional equilibrium only later, in the car.

'Would you mind telling me how we can expect to maintain a platonic friendship when neither of us can keep our hands off the other?' she asked practically.

He smiled to hear it spoken aloud, still unused to Ruth's straightforward approach to everything in life. 'We'll try harder,' he answered.

She closed her eyes briefly in frustration, and tried to change the subject. 'I'm nervous about meeting the architect,' she confided, anxious to re-route her thoughts to something other than his nearness. Confined as they were in the small car, she could reach out and touch him by moving her hand only a few inches. Just a bit to the left, and the long muscle of his thigh would tense beneath her hand, and while he drove, he could do nothing to stop her. Her fingers tensed and trembled as she resisted the impulse, forcing herself to remember a woman who had suffered so much for this man; but in a moment, her fingers would move of their own accord, and then . . .

'Don't be. I think you'll like his work.'

She frowned, trying to remember what she had said; what he was talking about.

'He's brilliant,' he continued. 'A genius in his own way, and I don't grant titles like that lightly.'

The architect. He was talking about the architect.

'He hasn't had an easy time of it, though. No self-respecting firm will hire him. He's a little too . . . eccentric for their conservative images. So he's been trying to make it on his own, with little success.'

'Who recommended him?'

Hampton made a sound of contempt and his lip curled. 'No one. No one I know has the perception to see exactly what the man is. I saw his house on the way upstate last month, banged on his front door to ask who had designed it, and hired him on the spot.'

She felt the brush of his eyes as he glanced her way.

'He's a bit . . . hostile,' he said hesitantly. 'Doesn't trust anyone, or like anyone, as far as I can tell. Try not to be put off by him too much. If you two can tolerate each other long enough, I think between you, you'll build one hell of a house.'

'You make him sound so forbidding. I feel like I'm about to go into battle,' she complained, and he chuckled.

'You may be right. You're two of the most stubborn people I've ever met. I think I'm almost going to enjoy watching the proverbial irresistible force meet the immovable object.'

The reservations Hampton's description instilled in Ruth intensified when she saw a tall, gaunt young man rise as they approached a corner booth in the dimly lit restaurant. When she drew closer, the image of youth fled in the sharply drawn lines of bitterness pulling down the cruel mouth, the deep hollows in the cheeks, and the dark, smudged shadows under his eyes. He pushed nervously at the black swatch of hair that lay across his forehead, and glared at her suspiciously from under hooded brows.

The man was a series of glaring contradictions: a pale, almost pallid complexion against hair so black it reflected blue in some places; a youthful innocence just barely hinted at beneath the cold, cynical expression; and a bright, blinding intelligence shining out through black eyes so intense they seemed to glitter with madness. He held out an angular hand with long, sensitive fingers as Hampton introduced them.

'Ruth Lyons, please meet Elliot Shore.'

She jerked her hand to a stop inches away from his. 'Elliot Shore?' she echoed incredulously. 'The Windom House?'

The suspicion intensified in his narrowed dark eyes, and he pulled his hand away. 'So the lady reads the society columns,' he said bitterly, and slumped back into his seat.

'Society columns?' she repeated, letting a broad smile flood her face. 'I don't know anything about that. What I do read is *Architectural Review*. That's where I saw the Windom House. Martin showed it to me. He was your greatest fan, you know.'

'Martin who?' he mumbled, showing such a profound lack of interest that the words barely registered as a question.

'Martin Westchester,' she said, slipping in beside him, forgetting Hampton's existence for the very first time in over a month. 'Lord, how we tried to track you down after seeing those elevations! We were like a couple of kids chasing after a movie star,' she laughed, then suddenly sobering, she shook her head. 'No one seemed to know where you were. And then . . .'

He looked at her coldly, and she thought immediately of a human skull left to dry in the desert air. 'And then the architectural reviews of Windom House followed the article, and Windoms sold it for one-tenth its value just to avoid the embarassment of living in such a white elephant, and Elliot Shore slipped back into oblivion where he belonged.' He nearly spat out the words, then his mouth curved in the cruellest smile she had ever seen, and he asked sarcastically, 'Tell me, Miss Lyons. What did you think of the Windom House? Did you think it was "original", "astounding", or simply outrageous?'

Ruth frowned in dismayed confusion. 'It was the most magnificent building I'd ever seen,' she answered quietly. She had delivered the accolade with such matter-of-fact sincerity that Shore's rigid defences dissolved, and she saw his face unguarded for the first time, and thought it was beautiful.

'Martin said the critics would crucify you,' she whispered, laying her hand over his, her face reflecting concern and a passionate empathy. 'And they did, didn't they? You shouldn't have had to stand against that alone.'

His eyes held hers with a questioning wonder, then a genuine smile touched his mouth and brightened his face, and he looked immediately like a young boy. 'Did you know Martin Westchester?' he asked slowly, devouring her with his eyes, as if he were afraid she would disappear if he looked away. 'I used to worship him—his work, actually. Some of his earlier designs were part of a graduate course I studied.'

'I was his assistant for five years; and yes, I knew him very well.'

Hampton leaned back in the booth across from the two young artists, watching their conversation accelerate into rapport, his eyes narrowed with thought. They seemed to feed on one another like interchangeable power sources, the brightness of one reflecting in the eyes of the other; and while part of him resented their ease and their obvious delight in discovering one another, part of him wanted to cherish them both, protect them from a world which would not understand such innocence.

'Champagne,' he directed the wine waiter, and while he specified brand and vintage, Ruth's eyes flashed gratitude that he recognised a cause for celebration when he saw one.

They finished the bottle before food they could not remember ordering arrived magically; then devoured it with gusto none could recall to equal it. The three of them conversed with the ease of people who had been friends for years, each of them thinking privately that food had never tasted so good, an atmosphere had never been so perfect, and time had never been as well spent as the last two hours.

'Where do you have to go now, Hampton?' Ruth asked peevishly, alluding to a schedule that rarely allowed for more than two hours in any one place.

'Absolutely nowhere,' he smiled. 'Today I'm a free man. Any suggestions?'

She and Elliot glanced at each other, said, 'The site,' simultaneously, then burst out laughing.

Hampton smiled and rose from his chair. 'Where else?'

Ruth and Elliot chattered constantly during the hour-long drive, exchanging ideas in a flurry of talk that was punctuated continually with exclamations of mutal delight. Hampton, who had brought the two intense, solemn young people together, could only marvel at the transformation one had worked upon the other, making them both behave like excitable children. He listened silently to the creative give and take of shared artistry, almost parentally proud that he had been the instrument to draw these two great talents together.

When they arrived at the site, Elliot scrambled from

the car, dashing to the edge of the hill as if he would leap out into space. He was like a small boy, free at last to express the limits of youthful exuberance, away from the watchful eyes of adults who would never understand. That he felt such freedom in the presence of Ruth and Hampton was a statement of such extraordinary trust that Ruth loved him instantly, and the narrow circle of her emotions widened to make room for Elliot.

'I don't think I've ever seen anyone so openly glad to be alive,' she mused. 'Did giving him this house do that?'

'Partly. He hasn't worked since the Windom house,' Hampton said, watching Elliot with a smile that was almost paternal. 'But it's more than that, I think. I think he was very lonely, and we—you and I—have alleviated that. He sees something in us that matches something in him. I don't know what, exactly; but I feel it too.'

Some people live their entire lives without ever feeling it, Ruth thought. Without ever experiencing that instantaneous, magical bond that springs to life so quickly between certain people that others can hardly believe it's real. And within the space of one week, you have felt it twice.

She got out of the car quietly and stood next to it, her eyes wandering over the meadow, remembering the last time she was here.

'You've never looked so beautiful,' Hampton said softly from the car's other side, and she turned her head to look at him. If his hair did not fall across his forehead in just that way, if his eyes were not so piercing and intent, if his shoulders were not so broad or his arms so strong then, perhaps, it wouldn't hurt so much. But somehow, she didn't think so.

'Hampton!' Elliot called out.

The imperiousness of the cry made Ruth smile. 'He calls you Hampton, too?'

He shrugged impatiently, then grinned. 'You're both impertinent. What is it, Elliot?' he called as the younger man approached at a jog.

'It would help if I knew your fiancée,' Elliot complained. 'I design for people, you know, not just sites.'

'This house will be mine,' Hampton said steadily, his eyes on Ruth. 'My wife-to-be will never live here. Design it for me.' There was a sudden tightening around his eyes, and he shifted his gaze to Elliot. 'Better yet, design it for us. The three of us. It should be our house anyway; yours, mine, and Ruth's. That's who it will really belong to, isn't it?'

Ruth and Elliot both stared at him, their eyes soft and full of wonder, and all three of them felt simultaneously the quiet joy of belonging.

Elliot's gaze shifted to Ruth, then back to Hampton, and his eyebrows raised only slightly before he moved off happily to scout every inch of the small meadow.

'Have I said it plainly enough?' Ruth asked quietly. 'That I love you?'

'You don't have to.'

'Yes, I do. Even if I never have a chance to say it again. Just this once, here, I have to say it out loud. I love you, Hampton.'

His eyes never wavered from hers, and his voice was strong and sure. 'And just this once, I'll say it. I love you, Ruth.' Then his voice faded to a whisper and his brow furrowed in anguish. 'More than life.'

CHAPTER FIVE

'HEY! Firetop!'

Ruth twisted on the ladder to grin down at the unshaven face of Sam Benedict, her construction foreman. Everything about the man was massive, including his voice, likened by the men who worked under him to the sound of a chainsaw just starting up. He had left school at twelve, an appalling lack of manners, and a sensitive nature completely contradictory to his rough, brawling exterior. He was one of those simple, honest, hardworking men that reaffirmed Ruth's belief that there were a lot of good things to be said about the human race.

'Break time already, Sam? I just got up here.'

'No,' he said slowly, tipping his head back to peer up the ladder. 'The Man is here.'

Ruth's heart skipped a beat and she tightened her grip on the ladder. 'The Man' was Hampton, and she hadn't seen him in three days, since the first meeting with Elliot.

'So tell him to come on in, Sam,' she said steadily. 'I want him to take a look at this ceiling moulding anyway. It should come down.'

Sam shifted his considerable weight nervously from one foot to the other, and looked over his shoulder once before whispering up at her, 'There's too much blocking the corridor for him to get in here. He's got a lady with him. In a wheelchair.'

Ruth felt her heart fall out of her body and tumble down the ladder without her. She had known this day would come, that eventually she would come face to face with the woman he would marry; but she'd been too busy, too comfortable with things as they were, to prepare for it. Now that the time was at hand, she scrambled through her thoughts for an excuse to avoid it.

'You okay, Firetop?' Sam's heavy brows came together at the top of his nose. A little slow in some things, Sam was a wizard at discerning the subtle nuances that revealed a person's shifting moods. It was part of the reason he was such an excellent foreman. More than once Ruth had seen him anticipate his workmen's objections before they were voiced, and change the tone of his own commands to forestall a rising rebellion. He was practising his perceptive magic on her now, and there was no way she could conceal her despair from those gentle, probing eyes. 'What is it, Ruth?' he asked gently, using her given name for the very first time.

'I'm fine, Sam. Just fine,' she lied, moving down the ladder on leaden feet. 'Where are they?'

Sam led the way to the large entryway, blocking Ruth's view with his broad back, stepping aside at the last moment with a worried glance at his boss. She forced a thin smile and nodded at him, and he disappeared into a side room.

Ruth stopped dead in the open space, staring through the haze of cement dust dancing in the morning sunlight to meet Hampton's eyes. For the moment, she could look only at him. He gave her a brief smile of mutual misery, conveying apology and regret and respect all at once.

'Good morning, Miss Lyons,' he said stiffly, then inclined his head towards the wheelchair at his side. 'May I present my fiancée? Miss Christie Taylor, this is Ruth Lyons.'

Ruth pulled her eyes from his reluctantly and walked towards the wheelchair, an artificial smile on her face, her eyes trying to focus on the slight form in the chair. She saw only a vague shape, and nothing more.

'I'm so pleased to meet you, Miss Lyons,' a light, musical voice said, and the shape swam into a distinct form before her eyes. 'Tray has had nothing but praise for your work, and I've been so anxious to see what you've done so far.'

She was without question the most beautiful woman Ruth had ever seen, and without the wheelchair to support Hampton's story, she would never have believed that that face had once been a ruin. Dark, glossy hair was swept back into an immaculate swirl, accentuating the fine, pronounced bone structure, the lively blue eyes, the nearly translucent complexion. Ruth had hoped desperately, although subconsciously, to see evil incarnate when she was finally forced to look upon this face; but it was totally without guile, open and trusting, and radiant with the inner peace Hampton had tried so hard to describe.

'Is there something wrong, Miss Lyons?' the lovely voice enquired politely, and Ruth realised she had been staring.

'I'm sorry,' she said quickly. 'I'm being very rude. It's just that you're so lovely. It took me by surprise.'

Finely arched brows raised slightly, startled to hear such artless, obviously genuine flattery from another woman. 'How kind of you to say so,' she replied graciously, somewhat taken aback by Ruth's straight-forwardness.

She shifted the upper part of her body in the chair by bracing slender arms on the rails, and Ruth winced with pity for anyone so cruelly confined. As much as she had wanted to hate this woman, compassion obliterated any envy. She felt a deep, wrenching pain to realise once and for all that Hampton was lost to her forever, and that she would not even have the satisfaction of despising the person who kept them apart.

'I'm afraid it will be difficult for you to see much of the house today, Miss Taylor,' she apologised. 'We didn't expect you, and the corridors are blocked with equipment and debris.'

'Please call me Christie,' she insisted with a lovely smile, 'and don't apologise. Tray warned me that I wouldn't be able to see much today, but I did so want to see the plans. He refuses to let me look at them without you present to explain the details.' She sighed with feigned exasperation and took Hampton's hand lightly in hers. 'As a matter of fact, he's been putting me off for so many days, that if I didn't know better, I'd think he was afraid to let me see the designs.'

Ruth looked sharply, if briefly, at Hampton, then returned her gaze to the appealing face beneath her. 'I hope that's not the case,' she responded with a thin smile. 'The design boards are set up in the library. If you follow me, I'd be happy to show them to you.'

Even with Hampton's previous warning that Christie would hate her plans, Ruth had no compunction whatsoever about showing them to her. Far from being the fire-breathing antagonist she had hoped for, this frail, charming woman hardly seemed capable of voicing disagreement, let along acting upon it. In a way, Ruth was sorry when Christie's polite attention revealed all too clearly that Hampton had been right, and the designs were not what she would have selected herself. For some inexplicable reason, Ruth had wanted to please her.

'Tell me, Ruth—may I call you Ruth?'

'Of course.'

Christie smiled her thanks. 'Did you see the foyer plan I had prepared?'

Ruth caught her lower lip between her teeth and frowned in evident consternation.

'Oh, come now!' Christie laughed gaily. 'I think we can be honest with one another. Besides, you have no choice. Your thoughts appear on your face whether you speak them aloud or not. You didn't like it at all, did you?'

Ruth sighed and spoke reluctantly. 'No. I'm afraid I didn't.'

Hampton's gaze shifted back and forth between the two women apprehensively.

'Thank you for your honesty, Ruth,' Christie went on, nonplussed. 'Although our tastes may differ, I think we can at least respect those differences in each other. I'm sorry to say I don't care for your designs much more than you cared for mine; but since Tray is absolutely inflexible about using your plans, it would seem you are the victor in this round.'

She tempered her words with a disarming smile, but Ruth still took a step backward at the force of the implied challenge, balking at the implication that she was an antagonist to a helpless, wheelchair-bound woman.

'That's a peculiar thing to say, Christie,' Hampton put in abruptly, stepping between the chair and Ruth as if he would protect one woman from the other. 'You chose the house, knowing I hated it. The agreement was that I would select the interior design, and that's what I've done. Miss Lyons has no part in this personally.'

'Of course, Tray,' Christie's voice was instantly apologetic. 'I never meant to imply that she did. Ruth?' She peered around Hampton's body and blinked engagingly. 'Please forgive me if I sounded spiteful. I've been terribly spoiled, you know; having everything in life exactly as I've wanted it for so long that I've forgotten how to compromise.'

There was something decidedly wrong about that statement that eluded Ruth for the moment.

'Your designs are lovely, of course,' Christie continued, taking in the series of drawings with a wide sweep of her hand. 'Very bold, and daring; much like yourself, I imagine. They may not be exactly what I had in mind, but I should certainly be able to compromise on such a small matter. Tray has given me so much already.'

There it was again. That definite discordant note in her words, as if they should have been delivered with bitter sarcasm. Yet her expression was sincere, her smile genuine, her discomfiture obvious. Ruth felt the reluctant stirrings of admiration for a woman who could sacrifice for the man she loved on a matter as important as the home she would live in. As soon as her mind had articulated that thought, Ruth frowned in open confusion. That was it, she realised, the glaring contradiction between Christie's words and her delivery. First she had implied that her life had been so idyllically perfect that it had spoiled her, when in fact she had suffered horribly for the past fifteen years. Then she had described the house's interior design as a 'small matter', when it should have been battle-worthy for any woman. She furrowed her brows in concentration, looking for the elusive point she was missing, trying to understand.

Christie's rose-coloured lips puckered in an appealing pout. 'Oh dear; I have offended you, haven't I, Ruth? I can see by your expression that you're very put out, and of course, you have every right to be.' The lovely face shifted subtly into an eloquent plea. 'I have absolutely no taste at all; think of it that way. Someone as ignorant of design as I am can't be expected to know excellence when I see it. Perhaps you can forgive me my thoughtlessness on those terms.'

Ruth was horrified by the evidence that this poor woman was so repentant she was near tears. 'I'm not at all offended,' she reassured her quickly. 'Just confused. I can understand that not everyone finds the same designs appealing, I just can't understand how anyone could consent to live in a house they didn't like with barely a protest, as you just did.'

Christie smiled benignly, and pressed Hampton's captive hand to her cheek. 'I want Tray to be happy,' she said artlessly. 'That's all that matters to a woman in love, isn't it?'

Ruth walked them to the outer door and stared after them as they left, disturbed by a vague unease.

'Bad vibes,' Sam's voice rasped next to her, and she jumped.

'What?'

'Bad vibes. That woman's full of them. Who is she?'

'She's Mr Hampton's fiancée, Sam.'

He barked a short laugh and slapped his side. 'I won't buy that one. The Man isn't stupid.'

'Whatever do you mean by that?'

Sam's lips twisted in a patient smile that made her feel about ten years old. 'Now why would a man marry a woman that hates him that much?' he asked.

'Hates him? Sam, you're crazy! She's been in love with him for years. And besides that, she's a lovely woman, devoted to Hampton; you can't imagine what she's suffered for his sake.'

'I can imagine that if anyone ever made that woman suffer, she'd give it back in spades,' he said gruffly, then reached out shyly to touch Ruth's hand. 'Your problem is you're too damn good to know bad when you see it. I hope for his sake that that man of yours has better eyes than you do.'

He stomped away down the corridor, leaving Ruth standing there in startled confusion. Eventually it struck her that Sam had referred to Hampton as her man, and she smiled sadly, wondering if it was that obvious to everyone.

Elliot was waiting at her apartment door for the second night in a row, brown grocery sacks lined up against the hallway wall at his feet.

Ruth brightened when she saw him, and greeted him with a hug he returned with equal warmth. 'That does it, Elliot. I'm having a key made for you, and you're moving in. At least until we get The Summit underway.'

There was no romantic allusion in the invitation. They had worked until well past midnight on the plans the night before, and Elliot had still faced the two-hour drive to his house upstate.

'You won't get an argument from me,' he grinned agreeably. 'Especially since nights are the only time you have free to work. I nearly fell asleep twice on the way home last night.'

For the second time, Elliot proved himself a remarkably innovative cook, puttering happily in the kitchen while Ruth showered and changed.

'What can I do?' she asked, padding into the kitchen in bare feet and an oversized, shaggy robe.

'Sit down,' he ordered. 'There's a drink ready on the table. You're the one with two jobs, so I'll be the happy homemaker. Besides, I can't stand anyone in the kitchen when I'm working. Drives me crazy.'

Ruth sank tiredly into a chair, totally content to be pampered and idle while Elliot prepared their meal.

He was sautéeing colourful bits of food in a sauce of some sort, and the fragrance alone made Ruth salivate. 'Two nights of you cooking and already I respond like Pavlov's dog,' she said happily. 'However do you expect me to readjust to canned spaghetti and crackers?'

'Ugh. You actually ate that stuff?'

'And will again, unless you're willing to stay on as permanent cook.'

He flashed a dark, direct glance in her direction. 'Don't extend any invitations you don't mean, Ruth.'

She hesitated before swallowing a portion of her drink in an audible gulp, startled by the implication in his words, and the magnetic power of his eyes. They were dark and brooding, so different in appearance, yet so similar in expression to Hampton's that she caught her breath.

'It's the very first time you thought of us that way, isn't it?' he asked steadily. 'As a man and woman?'

Her response was a weak exhale. 'Yes.'

'I thought so. Your invitation to move in was pretty casual.'

'Elliot, I . . .'

'Never mind. Don't say anything. Don't even think about it. Not yet. We'll play this one by ear.'

He turned back to the stove, his lips curved in a sensual smile, and Ruth downed the whole of her drink in one tip of her glass, subconsciously seeking fortification from any available source.

She watched him warily from under lowered brows, acutely aware of his physical attraction as a man. She noticed little things she had not seen before: the straight, finely shaped nose jutting nobly from the broad brow, the crisp slash of lips that were incredibly sensual despite their thinness, the high, patrician cheekbones that gave his face an ascetic aspect. His hands moved skilfully at his task, and she knew intuitively that whatever Elliot chose to do, he would do well.

His body was inclined slightly forward, giving the impression of high energy held barely in check, and for the second time within minutes, she made an involuntary comparison to Hampton. They both shared that same air of controlled power; that distinctly masculine characteristic of physical strength contained by the bright reins of intellectual force.

'How old are you, Elliot?' she asked suddenly, completely deceived by the uncanny ability of his face to shift expression within an instant, looking incredibly young at one moment, infinitely wise and experienced the next.

'Thirty-two. Why?'

'Just curious. It's impossible to tell with you. You could be sixteen, or sixty. I've never been sure which.'

'And is thirty-two a respectable age?' He set a plate laden with aromatic wonders in front of her, then set his own place and sat down.

'You never married,' she stated matter-of-factly, wondering how many women existed that could deal with the quicksilver temperament of this man.

'No,' he said between mouthfuls, pausing reflectively. 'No time, no money, no woman willing to put up with me, for that matter. The general consensus is that I'm subject to dark, terrible moods.' He grinned disarmingly, dispelling such a notion with the white flash of perfect teeth. 'How about you?'

Ruth tasted the dish before her, and raised her brows in surprise. 'This is fantastic, Elliot. What is it?'

'Japanese wizardry,' he shrugged with affect modesty. 'Are you avoiding the question?'

'No, of course not. There was never much time for anything but work with me either, that's all. Besides, I think I've always intimidated most men. They seem to shy away from me after a time.'

'What about Martin Westchester?' he asked intently. 'You were involved with him, weren't you?'

Ruth's face lifted in unabashed amazement, then she laughed. 'You mean sexually? Oh, Elliot! I loved Martin completely, without reservation. I would have stepped in front of a moving train if he'd asked me to, I trusted him that much. But Martin was eighty-three when he died.'

Elliot's dark brows shot upward. 'You're kidding! From what Hampton said ...' then his mouth clicked shut abruptly.

'What did Hampton say?'

Elliot shrugged and made a face. 'That you were carrying a torch for a dead man, that's all. The clear implication was that you had been lovers.'

Ruth sighed and nodded with a tiny smile of remembrance. 'Oh. I suppose he might have jumped to that conclusion. I never thought to define my relationship with Martin.'

'I assumed Hampton knew everything there was to know about you,' Elliot said levelly. 'You two give the impression of having known each other forever.'

'Two weeks,' she said. 'You met him before I did.'

Elliot's eyes narrowed during a long pause, and Ruth

had the uncomfortable feeling that he saw too much. 'I see,' he said simply.

The harsh jangling of the telephone interrupted them just as they cleared the table for work.

'Ruth.' The word came across the wires as a flat statement, not a question, and stopped her breath when she heard it. It was spoken as an incredible release, as if the man who uttered it needed desperately to hear it said aloud.

'Yes,' she breathed. 'I'm here.'

Elliot's eyes flashed upward at the tone of her voice.

'I just wanted to hear your voice,' Hampton said. 'After today.'

'I understand,' she murmured, wondering if his agony could match hers. 'It hasn't changed,' she added. 'Nothing has.'

There was a long pause at the other end, and she squeezed her eyes tightly closed, trying to picture him as he must look now; light hair ruffled, the lines of strain tugging at the strong features, lips compressed into a straight line of control.

'Good night, Ruth,' he said quickly, and abruptly broke the connection.

She replaced the receiver with an odd, stiff movement of her head, staring at the telephone as if it had been a living thing, just recently deceased. When she turned away from the 'phone, Elliot was standing directly in front of her, concern pulling at his brows.

'Anything you want to talk about?' he asked gently. 'I can be a great listener.'

His tenderness, his obvious caring, caught her off-guard, and she felt a lone tear slide from one eye before she could stop it. She touched his lips lightly with one finger as if to silence him, and smiled. 'I'll remember that,' she whispered, 'if I should ever need one.'

CHAPTER SIX

ELLIOT insisted on going to work with her the next morning. She wasn't certain if this was a residual protective instinct after seeing her so vulnerable the night before, or if he was simply curious about the house she had described with such distaste. Whatever the reason, he could not be dissuaded, and she gave him a preliminary tour, ending at the design boards in the library, where Sam came upon them.

His sharp old eyes narrowed suspiciously at the newcomer, and Elliot returned his stare with equal wariness.

'This is Elliot, Sam,' Ruth smiled. 'Remember? I told you about him.'

Sam's face cleared slightly, shifting into an expression that clearly said he would make his own judgement. 'Glad to know you,' he said curtly, and Elliot nodded a silent acknowledgment.

Ruth looked from one man to the other, puzzled by the subdued air of hostility between them. 'Elliot's just here for the tour, Sam. He's staying at my place until we get the plans for The Summit underway.'

Sam moved his bulk with surprising agility to stand between Ruth and Elliot, flashing an unmistakable challenge at the younger man.

Realisation struck Elliot with a sudden impact, and a smile broke across his features. The old man was obviously every bit as protective of Ruth as he was. For a strong, independent woman, she seemed to be inspiring a lot of the protective male instinct in the men around her.

'That woman is here again,' Sam said over his shoulder to Ruth, an obvious contempt lacing his words. 'She wants to see you in the conservatory.'

'But . . . I didn't see Hampton's car,' Ruth balked.

'He didn't bring her. She's here with some swank decorator. They've been buzzing over fabric samples for the last hour.'

Ruth opened her mouth to say something, then changed her mind. She had a clear mental picture of the furnishings that would complement the living quarters for Hampton, but realised she had no right to suggest them. Besides, he may have asked Christie to furnish the room.

'All right, Sam. Thanks.' And then to Elliot's puzzled expression, 'Come on, Elliot. You wanted to meet her. Now's your chance.'

Christie's chair was braked before the wide bank of windows, back to the door. When Ruth and Elliot walked in, she and a short, balding man were holding a length of heavy printed fabric between them, assessing the amount of light that filtered through it.

'Good morning, Christie,' Ruth said from across the room, trying to force lightness into her voice. She heard Elliot's sharp intake of breath when the lovely face turned to smile at them.

'Ruth!' Christie's voice rang with genuine pleasure, and her face shone with the radiance of a delighted child greeting her best friend. 'Now Mr Stanfield,' she said to the man next to her, dropping her end of the material with casual indifference; 'we'll have an expert opinion. Ruth's taste is flawless.' Her eyes sparkled like fire in blue ice as she looked Elliot up and down in fleeting, expert appraisal, then her smile blossomed. 'What a magnificent couple you make!' she said, clapping her hands. 'Assuming this is the lucky man in your life, I compliment you on your taste, Ruth. He's absolutely magnificent.'

'No, Christie,' Ruth put in quickly, deciding in that instant, without knowing why, not to mention The Summit. 'This is Elliot Shore. A friend. Elliot, Christie Taylor. Mr Hampton's fiancée.'

The dainty smile broadened and took on a new quality as Christie offered a slender, elegant hand. 'Hello, Mr Shore. You're a friend of Tray's then?'

'I hope so,' Elliot replied with a stiffness that made Ruth glance up at him curiously. His eyes were bright with appreciation for the beautiful creature who held his hand captive; but his expression was guarded.

'Tray does seem to collect the most beautiful people,' Christie sighed, her eyes fastened firmly on Elliot's. Then she dropped her hand gracefully and picked up a corner of the fabric lying across her lap. 'What do you think, Ruth? I'm at my wit's end, trying to find a fabric that will suit this room, and I do want Tray to be pleased. Would this do, do you think?'

Ruth quelched a grimace of distaste, and said carefully, 'The print seems a bit large for upholstery, Christie.'

'Oh no. Not upholstery. This is for the draperies.'

'Draperies?' Ruth echoed stupidly; then more strongly, 'Draperies? There won't be drapes in this room. The windows will be bare, just as they are. That's why we're preserving the moulding around them.'

Christie's delicate features puckered in a stricken frown. 'Really?' she asked, puzzled. 'Then . . . well, I'm afraid I don't know what Tray was talking about. He was absolutely adamant about complete privacy for this room when we discussed decorating it last night. Now why would he insist that that was my responsibility, when you'd already decided about the decor?'

Ruth pursed her lips in a disheartened expression that matched Christie's confusion. She and Hampton had never really discussed decorating this room, and he had obviously assigned Christie that task the night before. 'I'm . . . not sure,' she stammered. 'I may have misunderstood his intentions. If he told you to select material, well then . . .'

'Hampton would never block that view with drapes,' Elliot broke in decisively, and both women turned to him simultaneously, but he said nothing further.

'Well,' Christie said lightly, breaking the strained silence, 'listen to us, mystified by what Tray would want. I'll just ask him tonight, and if he wants drapes, we'll come back tomorrow. But if he does, Ruth, what colour do you think?'

'Something light,' Ruth said dully. 'And sheer. No pattern.'

'Of course,' Christie shook her head in a self-deprecating gesture, and frowned at the silent, uncomfortable form of Mr Stanfield. 'Really Mr Stanfield. You should have thought of that yourself,' she scolded him gently. 'But no matter. No harm done. Thank you, Ruth, for your help. I hope I haven't kept you too long from your work. Mr Shore?' She turned an apologetic countenance toward Elliot. 'Would you mind helping me up those two stairs? I'm afraid this chair gave Mr Stanfield quite a time on the way in.'

Elliot moved to roll the chair towards the steps that led down to the sunken room from the hallway. 'You'll need a ramp here, of course,' he said. 'I assume that's something that will be installed later.' He lifted the chair and the slight frame in it with almost no effort, setting it gently on the hallway's stone floor.

'I'm afraid I don't know about that,' Christie shrugged. 'I'm not an expert at reading plans, or elevations, or whatever you call them. Will there be a ramp, Ruth?' she asked over her shoulder.

'I'm sure there will be,' she replied softly, not sure at all. It occurred to her then that Hampton had never mentioned such a thing, and she wondered if the oversight had been intentional.

Christie spun her chair to face them both, smiling up at them with a childlike expression. 'Thank you both again, and you'll have to forgive me, but I must repeat: you two *should* be a couple. You're almost too perfect together to waste.'

She was gone with surprising rapidity for a chair-bound woman, forcing Mr Stanfield to trot behind, just to keep up with her. Elliot and Ruth stood silently, staring at the empty hall where she had been just a moment before.

'Well,' Sam's voice growled from behind them. He was developing the most irritating habit of appearing suddenly whenever Christie departed, as if he had been waiting to pounce, just out of earshot. 'What did she want today?'

'Drapes,' Ruth said absently, and tilted her head toward the conservatory. 'In there.'

Sam uttered a short, heartfelt oath. 'The Man won't have drapes in there,' he said definitely.

'Elliot seems to agree with you, but I'm not so sure . . .'

'Dammit, Ruth!' Elliot snapped. 'She plays you like a violin!'

She glanced up quickly at the darkening face, astounded by the harsh reprimand in his tone. She looked to Sam for defence, but the older man merely rocked back on his heels, beaming at Elliot like a teacher well-pleased with his student's keen observation.

'That's exactly right,' Sam affirmed. 'I tried to tell her that yesterday. That woman is an ill wind if ever I saw one.'

Elliot nodded in sage agreement, and Ruth looked from one to the other with amazement, bristling at the apparent conspiracy between these two men to slander a helpless woman behind her back.

'What's got into you two?' she demanded crossly. 'That poor woman has been nothing but nice to all of us, and you talk about her as if she were the devil incarnate; and what's worse, about me, as if I couldn't defend myself against her if she were!'

Sam and Elliot exchanged a look of knowing exasperation, increasing Ruth's irritation.

'Christie Taylor is a lovely woman,' she continued

vehemently, 'and the future wife of the man who employs you both. Think what you like, but keep your thoughts to yourselves. I won't hear anything more said against her!'

Sam shook his grizzled head and rolled his eyes at Elliot, who raised both brows in a helpless reply.

Ruth made a sound of frustration, and stomped away in a half-hearted show of temper, but heard Elliot's urgent whisper to Sam, and Sam's grunt of assent.

'Keep an eye on her, Sam, will you? She doesn't even know what she's up against.'

She resented Elliot's implication that she was naïve and helpless, and it showed in her terse, reserved comments at the apartment that night.

'What are you so damn mad about?' Elliot demanded when she ground a huge drawing sheet into a hard ball and flung it across the room.

'About your attitude!' she fired back. 'I heard the comment you made to Sam today about watching out for me, as if I were a stupid child, in need of a babysitter!'

Elliot took in the high flush of her cheeks with apparent indifference. 'That's a fair assessment,' he said drily, and she threw a pencil at him. It missed by a full yard, and he laughed at her impotence.

There was something infectious about Elliot's amusement; probably because laughter lifted his face into such a startling contrast to his normal expression of dark cynicism, or that intense, deadly serious look he wore when he worked. Because his face was beautiful when it relaxed with laughter, because she thought there had been precious little laughter in his life, Ruth didn't mind so much that his amusement was at her expense.

'We care about you, Ruth,' he said ingenuously. 'We just can't help ourselves, Sam and I.'

She smiled a tight, begrudging smile, but remained silent.

'Oh, come on, Ruth,' he teased, lifting her chin and smiling into her eyes. 'Lighten up. You know what your problem is? You're too serious. You don't have enough fun. All you do is work, work, work.'

'Listen to who's talking!' she accused him gently. 'When was the last time you did anything but scribble in that sketchbook of yours?'

He dazzled her with a boyish grin, then bent to peck her lightly on the nose. 'You know, I can't remember when it was. What do you say, Ruth? Shall the two drones put on clown suits and see how the rest of the world lives?'

So it was that an hour later, after fighting for turns in the shower like siblings, they were dressed and *en route* to one of the city's most fashionable nightclubs; Elliot in a black, pin-striped suit that accentuated his own brooding, mysterious darkness; Ruth in a long ivory sheath that dropped from one bare shoulder to fall in tiny pleats to the floor.

'She was right about one thing, you know,' Elliot had said as they stood side-by-side in front of the mirror before leaving the apartment.

'Who?'

'Christie Taylor. She was right. We're gorgeous together.'

Ruth had assessed their dual reflection with brows raised in amusement, and concluded that he was right. If relationships were ever judged by how well people looked together, she and Elliot would rate high marks indeed.

The club was pretentiously elegant, with small, intimate tables clustered like feeding sparrows around a large, highly polished dance floor. A multi-pieced orchestra played muted renditions of modern songs, geared down to suit the pompous, overdressed guests Elliot compared unfavourably to a gathering of narcissistic peacocks.

'Careful, Elliot,' Ruth chided him gently. 'Someday

these very people will be clamouring for your services as
an architect. You won't think so unkindly of them
then.'

'A peacock is a peacock is a peacock. That's how it
goes, isn't it? Or it is a peacock by any other name . . .'

There was a biting undercurrent of sarcasm in
everything he said about the surroundings, the people,
the orchestra; even the overpriced drinks. Ruth smiled
tolerantly as he ranted, understanding that this was his
catharsis; a release of all the bitter venom stored since
people just like those present had negated the worth of
his Windom house.

'Feel better?' she asked when he finally ran out of
commentary, and he grinned sheepishly.

'I do go on, don't I? Sorry.'

'It doesn't matter, Elliot. I don't blame you. Besides,
I want all that anger out of your system before we
dance.'

He looked out at the slow-moving couples sceptically.
'I'm a rock fan myself,' he said bleakly. 'I'm not sure I
can handle this ballroom stuff.'

'Pretend you're old and crippled and shuffling
somewhere,' she said playfully, pulling at his arm.
'You'll do fine.'

That Elliot was not a born dancer became painfully
obvious within the first sixty seconds on the floor.
Feeling her feet to be seriously at risk, Ruth stopped
him in mid-stride of what could have been either a very
shaky polka, or a very strong imitation of a beheaded
chicken. 'Stop,' she said, her hands pressing lightly on
his shoulders, her eyes seeking his.

'This is absolutely the only thing in the world I can't
do, Ruth,' he said miserably, at odds with himself for
failing at anything.

'Elliot, look at me,' she insisted, increasing the
pressure on his shoulders until his gaze shifted
reluctantly to meet hers. 'Now don't take your eyes off
mine,' she commanded in a husky monotone that

seemed to mesmerise him. 'Look at my eyes, and forget everything else. Only my eyes.'

Stirred by the sensuous purr of her voice, within seconds Elliot's total concentration was contained in the two pinpoints of light in dark eyes that bored into hers, and she felt the rest of his body relax. He began to move without thought, his body swaying unconsciously in time to the music. She followed him easily, her own slight form mirroring his with an inbred grace that set her long dress swaying in whispery undulations against her legs. His hands moved on her waist in response to the gentle flow of her hips, and Ruth felt his gaze intensify and sharpen until it held hers captive, and then she was the one who could not look away.

They moved slowly, languourously around a small area of the floor, staring into each other's eyes, oblivious of their surroundings. With her head lifted towards his, Ruth's hair tumbled down her back until wisps brushed against Elliot's fingers. He trembled at the sensation, a lock of his own black hair falling across his forehead unnoticed while his eyes burned beneath it.

When the music stopped, Elliot came to an abrupt halt, never taking his eyes from Ruth's. 'I think this has probably been the sexual highlight of my life,' he said hoarsely.

Ruth took a deep breath to still her own racing pulse, felt the tension in the muscles of her neck prickle as the moment passed, and forced a light laugh. 'And that's the secret to dancing,' she said almost too casually. 'It's open, public courtship, and totally sexual. I had a feeling you'd be good at it, if you ever let yourself go.'

His eyes darkened and narrowed, and she felt the heat of his breath stir the tendrils at her forehead. 'Ruth . . .' he whispered, but his words were lost in the lilting call of an unmistakable voice from a table close to the floor.

'Ruth! Elliot!'

They turned their heads in unison, looking like two children stopped in the midst of a dangerous game; their eyes wide and bright, their face flushed to a matching, rosy glow.

Christie lifted a graceful arm and waved them over to the table she shared with Hampton.

Ruth smiled woodenly as they approached the table, her eyes fastened on Christie, purposefully avoiding Hampton's gaze. Christie wore a low-cut, midnight blue silk with a dazzling cluster of diamonds suspended from an almost invisible chain. With every breath she took, the diamonds rode the generous swell of her breasts like a surfboard on a high, rolling wave, shooting back rays of multi-coloured light that caught the eye and drew it inexorably towards the cleavage straining at the fine, dark silk. The effect was startling, and a quick sidelong glance at Elliot confirmed that even he had fallen prey to the obvious design. Her hair was piled high on her head in a glossy mass of black curls, and she looked tenderly youthful, like a beautiful child playing dress-up.

'Sit down! Sit down, both of you!' she commanded merrily, catching Elliot's hand as he drew close, pulling him down into the chair next to hers. 'I couldn't have wished for a better evening, meeting you both here. It was hard enough convincing Tray to leave his work long enough for a little fun. Perhaps he'll brighten up now, with his friends here.'

Ruth risked a direct glance at Hampton and felt a familiar shudder when their eyes locked. His face was tight and angry, and his eyes narrowed with silent accusation.

'Really, Ruth,' Christie reclaimed her attention with the light touch of cold fingers on her arm. The pale blue eyes were alight with mischief; the rose of a mouth curved in a conspiratorial smile. 'And to think you tried to pretend you and Elliot were simply friends! Well, your secret's out now, you two. I don't think I've ever seen such an erotic dance in my life! Not that it was at all indecent,' she hastened to add, frowning in apparent concern that she might give offence. 'You barely touched each other, but still . . .' Her voice gave way to a wistful smile. 'It makes me long to dance again.'

Ruth's face puckered in sympathy; Elliot's stiffened with uncertainty; and Hampton's seemed devoid of any emotion whatsoever.

'I don't dance,' Elliot contributed to the awkward silence. 'Ruth was just teaching me.'

'Then she's a marvellous instructor,' Christie said with a delicate arch of one brow. 'Perhaps you could take Tray on as a pupil, Ruth. As I remember, he was a bit awkward on the floor years ago.'

Ruth glanced at Hampton's dark, unreadable expression once and flushed, shaking her head. 'I don't think . . .'

'Oh, please, Ruth,' Christie cajoled. 'I feel so guilty keeping poor Tray tied here to a table, while everyone else dances. As a favour to me? Please?'

'Perhaps Ruth has had enough dancing for one evening,' Hampton said stonily.

'Oh no. That is, I love to dance, if you'd like to . . .'

'There, you see? Now go on, you two. Elliot will keep me company.' Christie waved them away without another thought, and Ruth felt Hampton's hands behind her, waiting to pull out her chair.

The hand that cupped her elbow as he led her to the floor was cold and impersonal, as was his voice. 'Somehow I didn't picture you as a social butterfly; or Elliot either, for that matter.'

'And you were right,' she said tremulously, responding to his nearness in spite of his remote attitude. 'This was a lark, really. Elliot thought we should get away from work, and out of the apartment for one night.'

'Your apartment?' he asked airily, looking over her head with apparent disinterest.

He turned then to face her on the floor, and she tensed at the small space between their bodies, quivering with anticipation for the moment when he would take her into his arms. 'Hampton,' she whispered, her hands lifted in a prelude to the dance, her eyes wide and questioning.

He put one hand lightly against the small of her back, taking the one she offered in the cool, relaxed grip of his fingers. He moved immediately into the rhythm of the waltz with a grace that belied Christie's earlier comment, guiding her expertly across the floor, but holding her away from his body, refusing to look at her. 'You and Elliot work in your apartment?' he asked stiffly, and she frowned up at his coolness.

'Yes. At night, after I get home. He's staying with me until we complete the plans for The Summit.'

His only response was a tightening of the muscle in his jaw.

Ruth let herself go to the slow whirl of the cadenced dance, leaning back against his hand, looking up to devour his face with her eyes. Even now, avoiding her gaze, holding himself aloof as he must with Christie here, his power over her was complete. She stared up at the strong, squared jaw, the sweep of blond over his wide brow, the features that exuded confidence and an unquestionable, animal authority. Then his eyes dropped to hers in an angry glare, and she trembled in his arms and nearly stumbled.

'Are you in love with him?' he demanded unexpectedly. 'Or is it purely a sexual attraction?'

'What?' she breathed, astonished. 'You mean Elliot?'

His fingers tightened to a painful squeeze on her hand while his lips curved in a false, unpleasant smile. 'Of course, Elliot!' he hissed between his teeth, and she felt a jerk of sudden, uncontrollable fury from the hand on her back.

She realised at that moment how ludicrous the situation was. He, who had rejected everything she had offered, while binding himself irrevocably to another woman, was possessively jealous of her friendship with Elliot. Furiously, dangerously jealous. She could feel the restraint in hands she knew instinctively wanted to punish her, to break her to his will. Yet he had no right. Any claim on her emotions was totally unjust. While no man would ever move her as this one did, nor possess her completely as long as Hampton lived, anger at his unfair possessiveness shot to the surface.

Did he expect her to remain friendless, even loveless, while he married another?

She returned his frigid smile with one as cool, and wondered if bystanders could see the raging torrent seething between their false expressions. 'And what if I should be having an affair with Elliot?' she asked with saccharine sweetness. 'Just remember, Hampton, anything I give him was offered first to you, but you turned it down. Nobility is very expensive, isn't it?' It was a petty, childish impulse that made her encourage his suspicions, but she couldn't help herself.

His face darkened with the blind rush of fury, and he pulled his shoulders sharply forward as if he would double up with the pain of keeping it all safely contained. The music stopped then, and though his hand on her upper arm seemed casual to anyone who might be looking, his fingers pressed painfully into the soft flesh on the inside.

'You're hurting me!' she hissed quietly through a smile as they returned to the table.

'How very thoughtless of me,' he said sarcastically, and released her arm.

Hampton glared malevolently at Elliot through Christie's unaware chatter, and Elliot returned the look darkly, knowing only that Ruth's overly bright expression concealed a profound misery that had not existed before her dance with Hampton. He had a deep, abiding respect for this man, but to Ruth he was obligated by a more primitive, protective instinct. Between the two loyalties, there was no contest. He tossed a brief, questioning glance at Hampton's rigid features, then made their excuses aptly and led Ruth out to the car.

He respected her silence until they were back in the apartment; then he turned her towards him with an assertiveness that startled Ruth out of her miserable introspection. He shook her lightly, almost paternally, by the shoulders. 'I think it's time you told me what's going on here,' he said sternly. 'The only man I ever admired looked at me tonight like he wanted me dead, and left you cringing like a whipped puppy. I didn't know whether to ask him what I'd done, or deliver a right cross for whatever he'd done to you. Now what is it?'

'He thinks we're having an affair,' Ruth said dully, averting her eyes.

'And if we were?' he said with exaggerated softness, lifting her chin until she was forced to meet his eyes. 'What business would that be of his?'

Ruth hesitated, pressing her lips together. 'Let's just say ... he's a bit jealous of ... my affections.'

She thought she had seen anger in Elliot's face before. Even in repose, the tight, hard lines around his mouth had always spoken of a deep, destructive bitterness lying just beneath the surface. But now, as his cheeks hollowed with the force of his clenched jaw, as his eyes narrowed to glittering, black slits in a face suffused with red, she realised she had never seen Ellliot's rage before, and hoped she would never see it again. 'That bastard!' he hissed, unconsciously tightening his grip on her shoulders until she nearly cried out. 'That man pulled me out of hell,' he intoned, his words dripping like acid on a steel plate, 'but so help me, if he were here now, I'd kill him.'

'No, Elliot ...'

'Don't defend him, Ruth! He's beneath defence! He leads you on, expecting you to remain faithful while he flaunts another woman in your face . . .'

'Elliot!' Her voice rang sharply in the quiet apartment. She lifted her hands to clasp his arms, and felt the bulging tension in his biceps. 'He isn't leading me on, Elliot. He's been honest from the beginning.'

And then she had to tell him. To salvage his respect for Hampton; to preserve the bond that should exist between two men so very much alike; she had to tell him everything. Somehow during the telling they had drifted to the couch, and when Ruth had finally said it all, she felt Elliot's strong arms close around her. He held her close, soothing her with the tender movements of his hands stroking her hair, but his voice quivered when he spoke.

'Poor Hampton,' he said quietly, shaking his head. 'He's crazy, you know. Christie Taylor is not what she seems. She'll make him miserable, if she doesn't destroy him first.'

'You're wrong about her, Elliot. You and Sam are both wrong. She's sacrificed a great deal for Hampton. I think she's probably the most selfless woman I've ever met. I would have hated him, in her place.'

'That's what bothers me the most. That she doesn't. There's something twisted about her loving the man who ruined her life. Something basically, terribly wrong.'

'You're just too used to seeing the bad in people, Elliot,' Ruth said gently. 'When you meet a truly good one, you can't believe they're real.'

'No, Ruth.' He shook his head and smiled sadly down at her. 'You're wrong about that. I see the good in you, and in Hampton, and believe me, there's none of that in Christie Taylor. In fact, you two make a perfect target for a person like that. You're destroying yourselves. She doesn't even have to lift a finger.'

She tipped her head back in the circle of his arm to look up into his dark eyes, and saw the caring there.

'What a cynic you are, Elliot.' She smiled and pressed his cheek lightly with one hand. 'I almost wish I needed all that blustering protectiveness of yours, just so I could take advantage of it.'

He grabbed her hand and pressed his lips deeply into the hollow of her palm. 'You have it anyway, Ruth, like it or not.'

She let a long, shaky sigh release the last of the tension, and snuggled closer to the warmth of his embrace, feeling safe and sheltered for the very first time since Martin died.

CHAPTER SEVEN

No one had seen Hampton in nearly two weeks. 'Oh, he's off on business somewhere,' Christie had said airily when Ruth had finally mustered the courage to ask about him. 'And to tell you the truth, I haven't the slightest idea where he's gone or when he'll be back. I'm afraid in that regard at least, Tray is still very much his own man. Was it something urgent, Ruth? Shall I have his office try to reach him?'

'No. It will keep, Christie. Thanks.'

But she yearned for the sight of him. It was all she needed, she thought, to still the quiet ache that hovered where her heart should be. Their last words had been angry and cruel, and the spiteful satisfaction she had felt then to let him believe she was involved with Elliot, left nothing but a bitter residue. The senses he had awakened were like demanding fledglings, clamouring for constant feeding; and she found herself longing for the warmth of human affection from any source, just to fill the new void. Hampton could have stilled the need with a touch of his hand, or a deep glance from the grey eyes that reminded her she was his, and always would be. But Hampton had gone away, and the need lingered; and for every additional day he was gone, Ruth became more vulnerable.

This was the aching emptiness friends should fill, she thought. But the greatest irony in her life at this point was that of all the people she had grown suddenly close to, the person she saw most often was the woman standing between her and Hampton. Sally was constantly busy at the office, and Elliot, dear Elliot, had faded from her life as if he had never been there. He was gone in the mornings by the time she got up; off to the hill to sketch, he said in notes left on the kitchen table; but the light still vanished early from the sky, and Elliot never came home before midnight. She never knew where he went, and would never have intruded to ask, even if she'd seen him long enough to have the opportunity.

So life was suddenly, bleakly empty, and but for Sam's constant fatherly presence at the job site, she would have felt totally alone. Just as you were after Martin died, she reminded herself; right up to the day you met Hampton. It always seemed to come back to Hampton. He was the one who had started it all; jangling the sleeping emotions that cried for human affection, and made life bitter without it.

But Christie had not disappeared. In fact, Christie was always there; at first with the sheer, mint green fabric for the conservatory drapes. Ruth's heart had plummeted at that, because she had never really believed that Hampton would permit shrouding the lovely old windows. That Christie had appeared with the inoffensive fabric was irrefutable proof that he had, and Ruth felt somehow betrayed. After the windows had been measured and the material was safely in the hands of the seamstress, Christie found other excuses to linger at Hampton House. Eventually she ran out of excuses, and made a touching admission to Ruth.

'I know I must be underfoot, but I simply don't know what else to do with myself,' she said plaintively. 'You're really the only other woman I know in the States, and with Tray gone—well, I'm lonely.'

Ruth knew the feeling, and found herself sharing lunch with the beautiful woman more than once; comparing childhoods, discussing politics, or simply passing the hour in idle, meaningless conversation. Eventually she became used to Christie's presence, then grew to expect it, looking for her in the mornings as one looks for a stray puppy who comes regularly to beg for handouts.

'We're friends, aren't we, Ruth?' Christie asked on what would prove to be the last day of Hampton's absence. There was a soft, urgent plea in the question, a pathetic note, almost; but the blue eyes were strangely intense.

'Of course, Christie,' she answered automatically, sipping at her mid-morning coffee.

The thought was preposterous, of course and, in recalling it later, Ruth thought that they were not friends at all, and that their relationship was very strange indeed. They never shared confidences, for one thing; and as much as she racked her brain, in all the hours they had spent in each other's company, Ruth could not remember a single time they had laughed together. Nor had Christie ever mentioned Hampton, or her coming marriage, and although Ruth was secretly grateful for that, it seemed strange all the same. Had she been the bride-to-be, her conversation would have been full of it, but it never seemed to occur to Christie. Still, it was the lack of laughter that bothered her most of all.

'Hey, Firetop.' Sam's face peered around the doorframe into the room where she was working.

'Hi, Sam. Don't tell me you're finally going to find time to lunch with the boss. It seems like I haven't seen you in days, or sampled your wife's baking, either.'

'Huh? What're you talking about? I've always got time for the boss. There's just been somebody ahead of me in line lately, and my mother taught me never to pick a fight with a cripple.'

'Sam!'

'Never mind.' He shook his head impatiently. 'Elliot's waiting outside. He told me to deliver you if I had to carry you out. He wants to take you to lunch.'

'Elliot!' Her face brightened momentarily, then fell again. 'Oh, Sam. I can't leave today. They've just started in the conservatory, and . . .'

'I'll take care of the conservatory,' he interrupted

gruffly. 'And I'll carry you out if I have to, just like Elliot said, so you might as well go quietly.'

Suddenly Ruth felt very tired, and the thought of being carried anywhere by anyone sounded almost appealing. 'Okay, Sam,' she sighed. 'Consider me out to lunch. I think I need it.'

'I think you needed it a long time ago.'

She tried for a smile that came out as a weak grimace, shrugged, then left the house.

Elliot sat sideways in the front seat of his car, looking carefree and almost dashing in a loose black shirt and matching slacks. His hair had been ruffled by the wind and lay tangled across the unfamiliar deep tan of his forehead. It was obvious that he had spent most of the past two weeks outside in the sun, and the deep colour in his face made him look exotically foreign.

He took her chin in his hand and examined her face with an intent expression. 'You're working too hard,' he pronounced finally. 'You look tired.'

'A shower and a change of clothes will fix that,' she smiled. 'Where are you taking me?'

'Halston's-on-the-River. You game?'

'Game? I'm overdue. I haven't been there in years, and I love the place. But why all the sudden attention? You've been making yourself scarce for so long I was beginning to wonder if I lived alone.'

She had said it in light jest, but he took the tease seriously. 'I'll explain at lunch, Ruth,' he said sombrely.

'Oh, Elliot.' She reached across the seat to squeeze his hand affectionately. 'You don't have to explain. I know you've been preoccupied on the hill, and what you do between sunset and midnight is your own affair.'

He shot her a grin as he backed out of the drive. 'So you know when I get home, eh?'

'Of course I do. I don't fall asleep until I hear your key in the lock. You don't have an exclusive on worrying about friends, you know.'

He nodded, smiling, and they drove home in companionable silence.

For a reason Ruth could not surmise, Elliot insisted on waiting in the car while she showered and changed. She had been so long in the functional, unflattering coveralls that the prospect of dressing in something feminine was strangely exciting. What she had told Hampton that first day at the house had been true: she never dressed to please anyone but herself; but today her self-image needed a little nurturing, and the forest-green silk sheath was the perfect medicine. It slid over her body like water in constant motion, moving to catch the thrust of a full hip, or the long line of her thigh. The neckline dipped in a flattering vee that exposed a tantalising glimpse of full, high breasts. She slipped into slender heels that made her legs look longer still, caught her hair with a gold clip on top of her head, and nodded with satisfastion at her reflection. She felt good about herself for the first time in days; for the first time in two weeks, in fact.

Elliot was leaning back against the car when she came down, his legs crossed at the ankle. He looked up through a fringe of black hair and emitted a low whistle. 'I'd forgotten,' he said simply, opening the car door for her. It was an obvious allusion to the sudden reminder that there had been a woman beneath those baggy coveralls.

'Believe me, Elliot,' she answered gaily, 'so had I.'

The spring air, the short drive up the river road, and just being somewhere other than at work all acted like a tonic on Ruth. She knew that Elliot's presence had more to do with her lifted spirits than anything else, but whatever the reason, she was light-hearted and gay by the time they reached the restaurant. She almost clapped her hands in delight when they were led to a table abutting the stone wall on the terrace. From this vantage point they could see the river below twisting away in either direction, like a silver ribbon carving a path through a standing audience of budding trees.

'Oh, it's beautiful, isn't it!' she exclaimed.

'You're sure you won't be too cold out here?'

'Certainly not. The sun is lovely, and eating inside at Halston's is almost a sacrilege. Watching the river is my favourite part of the meal here.'

Elliot was strangely quiet as the waiter served a light, fruity wine, then left them alone to examine the menus. The view is wasted on him, Ruth thought, as she felt his eyes return again and again to her face.

'What is it, Elliot?' she asked finally, leaning across the small table to rest her fingers lightly on his closed fist. 'What's troubling you?'

He stared down at her hand curiously, studying it as if it were an alien life form he had never encountered before; then he lifted his head and smiled. 'Your eyes match your dress,' he said in a low voice. 'They're both the colour those trees down there will be in another week or so.'

'I didn't think you'd noticed the trees,' she replied. 'And your eyes match your shirt. They're shiny black and absolutely unreadable. Now what is it?' She squeezed his hand gently until the fist opened, turned, and closed again around her fingers.

'I stayed away as long as I could, Ruth,' he whispered.

'Stayed away?'

'From you. I thought you needed the time. I thought we both did.'

Her nostrils flared with a quick intake of breath as she read his eyes.

'Listen,' he said earnestly, leaning forward until she became aware of the faint, musky smell of aftershave rising from his body. 'We're a man and a woman, sharing the love of our work, mutual respect, and a very small apartment. What's more, we were both very vulnerable after that scene at the club with

Hampton. But I don't want vulnerability to be the reason we come together. I want it to be something more. So, I stayed away until it passed. Like I said, for as long as I could.'

There was no reason to pretend she didn't know what he was talking about. She'd felt the same physical stirrings in Elliot's presence as he obviously felt in hers. She would have been immune not to. He was virile, intelligent, caring, and possessed an animal magnetism so like Hampton's that her own responses had frightened her more than once. Although she had missed the comfort of his companionship for the last two weeks, there had been a secret relief, too, not to have to deal with his nearness.

'And now?' she asked simply.

He leaned back in his chair and looked up at her from under lowered brows. The gaze he levelled at her was masterful and infinitely masculine, and told Ruth the strength of the will that had kept him from her this long. 'And now I'm not trying any more. We'll go back to where we were, and let nature take its course. I'm tired of fighting it.'

She felt a sudden chill as a light breeze kissed the back of her neck, making all the tiny hairs there quiver. It was too direct; too open; this challenge of his. His meaning couldn't have been clearer had he sent formal, written notice that he intended to seduce her, if the spirit moved him. Yet the prospect didn't frighten her. She, too, was tired of fighting the forces building within her, clamouring for release. Tired of fighting the nagging, insistent needs of a passionate nature; the ache that Hampton had planted, that would only subside under the touch of a loving human hand. And Elliot was her friend. First and foremost, they were friends. If life held that they should be more than that, then so be it.

She shrugged in a lightning flash of nonchalance that came as an immediate relief, and with that gesture, the strain of the past two weeks slipped away. Her expression lightened, and her green eyes sparkled. 'Does this mean I won't have to eat canned spaghetti any more?'

Elliot released his own tension in a great laugh. 'Among other things,' he smiled, and in that instant, the wall between them crumbled, and they were easy with one another again.

'So where have you been until midnight each night, Elliot?' It was a knowing tease she would have delivered to any female roommate.

'Driving around; at the theatre; or in bars,' he replied easily. 'In bars, mostly.'

'Fighting off the attentions of this city's predatory females, no doubt.'

'Naturally,' he grinned.

Ruth believed him. Wherever he might go, Elliot's dark air of mystery was bound to attract women. She felt a lofty immunity to that obvious sexual appeal of his, one which weakened only in rare moments of physical closeness. The sense of immunity made her daring, with the security of the small table between them, and a watchful public as guardian of their behaviour.

'Have you ever been in love, Elliot?'

'Not before you.'

'And are you in love with me?' she smiled.

'I love you, Ruth,' he replied carefully.

'I know that. And I love you. But are you *in* love with me?'

He frowned uncertainly and lifted one shoulder in a barely discernible shrug. 'I'm not sure.'

As though that had been the last chain holding her back from complete freedom, Ruth lifted her chin and blew a long sigh out between lips curved in a beautiful smile. When she dropped her head, her face was alight with the confidence of one who sees everything in its proper perspective. 'Let's take a bottle of champagne up to the hill, Elliot. Maybe two bottles. I feel this incredible need to simply let go.'

There had been no conscious plan for an afternoon of careless frolic on the hill. And that was just as well, because Ruth wasn't dressed for it. Even if she had been, seeing Elliot's sketch would have shattered the mood anyway.

They were sitting next to each other at the edge of the bluff, sharing youthful recklessness and the second glass of champagne when Elliot flipped back over the cover of the sketchbook on his lap. Ruth's face shifted instantly from exuberance to reverence as she looked at the first drawing. She touched the dark pencil lines tentatively with one finger, as if she could feel the glass and wood that would eventually grow from those lines.

'Oh, Elliot,' she whispered, and then words failed her.

Elliot's face glowed with pride in his own achievement, and the satisfaction of knowing another human being understood the full extent of what his mind had created.

The house was an extension of the hill itself; rising in lines so pure and clean that their very precision was the only indication it was not a natural formation. The hill did not accommodate the house, the house accommodated the hill, blending into the environment as if it had every right to be there. It was wide at the base that sat on the broad meadow, narrowing as it soared up towards the sky in an imitation of the trees behind it. It was a hasty sketch, but bright with the promise of one man's mind, visible at last in the crisp black lines on a blank sheet of paper.

'It's incredible, isn't it?' Ruth murmured in awe. 'To be able to take an empty sheet of paper, and turn it into something so beautiful, with the power of a single thought.'

Elliot closed his eyes and shrugged in a gesture that mimicked false modesty. 'I didn't think it was so bad, either,' he said nonchalantly, then a wide grin broke on his face when Ruth poked him in the arm.

Suddenly her mind was racing with thoughts of the interior design, and she snatched the pad, flipped to a clean sheet, and began to sketch furiously.

'Like that,' she said intently, emphasising her words with the long stroke of a pen; 'and that, and that. So the outside timbers support this wall, and leave the entire span open for glass. See what I mean?'

Then they were both lost in the sketches, their minds flying on the same track, envisioning the best they both could do. For a time it seemed that they had no cumbersome bodies; that they were simply two bright spots of pure intellect, focusing thoughts that found form on the blank sheet of a cheap sketchbook.

They huddled close together, facing the bright spring sky, absorbed in the vision they were creating. Their heads touched as they bent over their work, dazzling in the contrast of Ruth's sunlit-red hair brushing Elliot's glistening black, the strands moving and mingling like a marriage of two spirits. From a distance they looked like two children, pressed together in irresistible enthusiasm, and this is how Hampton first saw them.

He approached them silently, and was only a few feet behind them when the sound of a twig underfoot finally penetrated Ruth's intense concentration. The two turned their heads together, cheeks brushing, they were so close; and they raised their eyes to Hampton—eyes bright with excitement, dancing above flushed cheeks. They looked young, and innocent, and achingly alive.

'I didn't expect to find anyone here,' Hampton said apologetically.

He looked so incredibly tall to Ruth, and omnipotent, standing there above them with his long legs spread slightly, looking down like a benevolent god at the children he had created. His loose white shirt billowed in the breeze, and the steady grey eyes reflected shades of blue from the facing sky. A thatch of blond angled across his forehead, lifted with the wind, then fell again, glistening with the golden sparks from a lowering sun.

Ruth took a deep, shuddering breath, and realised it was the first she had taken since seeing him.

Elliot sprang to his feet in a delayed reaction and extended his arm hesitantly. 'We've missed you,' he said when Hampton clasped his hand; and though Hampton raised one eyebrow in amused scepticism, Ruth knew Elliot's words had been sincere. No matter what feelings crossed swords between the two men because of her, the three of them were inexorably bound together, caught in the trying triangle of kindred spirits struggling to find their proper place.

She looked up at the two men joined by their hands, and was struck by the illusion which cloaked each one. Elliot, magnetic and mysterious, for all his brooding darkness was still light inside, relatively unmarred by life's experience, still innocent and open, like an expectant boy. Yet Hampton, golden and bronze, almost godlike in white, concealed with his light appearance a dark, tormented mind, scarred by misery and wounded by guilt. Enigmas, both; and Ruth felt the very separate loves she felt for each well up inside until she could barely contain them.

She looked up at Hampton with eyes that never expected anything but the truth, and asked plainly, 'Why did you run away, Hampton?'

He dropped Elliot's hand and shoved both of his deep into the pockets of his slacks. 'For the same reason most people run away, Ruth,' he said quietly, gazing down at her with eyes that never wavered. 'I was up against something I couldn't handle.'

Because he never denied running away, trying to mask the truth with the wide range of excuses available, Ruth and Elliot both knew he had made an admission of trust, and that the admission made him vulnerable. It was a seal on the friendship that drew them together.

'Where were you?' Elliot asked softly, and Hampton lifted his eyes with a weak smile.

'Everywhere. Nowhere. Alone, mostly.'

Ruth thought that they had all been alone since he left, and that maybe he was the bond that held them all together.

'We've all been alone.' She said it aloud, without thinking. 'And none of us liked it much. I don't think we should try it again.'

Hampton and Elliot laughed nervous little laughs that sounded so weak and silly, that they all laughed harder, genuinely, and the wounds that had pulled them apart were miraculously healed.

When they huddled together over the drawings later, Elliot anxious, Hampton rapt with silent, deep admiration, and Ruth drawing strength from the presence of both, she glowed with an inner warmth she had never experienced before, and wanted the moment to go on forever.

By sunset they had finished the champagne and exhausted their enthusiasm. A comfortable silence fell over them as they lay the drawings aside, and paused to watch the sun dip closer to the distant hills. But without the diversion of the plans, Ruth felt the crackle of tension touch her skin, and a sudden, blinding awareness of Hampton consumed her senses. She could see the golden hair of his forearm curled against the bronze skin just inches away, and felt a heavy weight descend on her chest and make her feel slightly light-headed.

'It's getting chilly,' she said suddenly, and both men turned towards her, stopping their mutual impulse to pull her into the warmth of their arms at the same instant. Their eyes met briefly, in a guilty acknowledge-ment that said many things. 'And it's past suppertime,' she went on, rising to her feet between them, feeling almost naked with her bare legs the only barrier between the two men.

Elliot rose smoothly, then stood in almost youthful awkwardness, not quite certain how to take leave from Hampton. But Hampton handled the moment with a mastery that was almost incidental. 'Ruth will ride with me,' he said simply, rising in a fluid movement to stand before Elliot, as if to say he knew he might be challenged. 'I have some apologies to make to her.'

Elliot's eyes darted uncertainly from Ruth's questioning expression to Hampton's grim look of authority. For a moment it seemed that he might protest, and Ruth almost hoped he would. Not because she didn't want to go with Hampton, but because it would have said something positive about Elliot, and how he really felt about her.

He stood quietly for a long moment, staring frankly at Hampton, then his eyes flickered briefly and he nodded. 'All right, then. I'll see you at home later, Ruth.'

Hampton watched silently until Elliot's car disappeared into the dusk, then turned and stared out across the darkening sky and spoke without looking at her. 'If it had been me, I never would have left here without you.'

He turned his head slightly, and their eyes met in the deepening twilight; then Ruth looked away, unable to face him and speak at the same time.

'I've never liked tragedies,' she said softly. 'Starcrossed lovers and all that nonsense. I hate stories like that.'

'It's the ones with happy endings that are stories,' he said from beside her. 'More often than not, it's the tragedies that reflect reality. Maybe that's why you don't like them.'

It sounded more like a philosophical discussion from her college days than a conversation about their real lives, and maybe that was just as well. It made it easier to say it all aloud. 'No,' she said thoughtfully. 'That's not the case. I've never run from reality, but I still believe that people make their own happiness—and their own sorrow—and that the victims of most tragic love stories aren't really victims at all. They're perpetrators.'

He chuckled without humour. 'The old you-made-your-bed-now-lie-in-it theory?'

She spun quickly and matched his curious stare with steady eyes. 'That's it exactly. Life is what we make of it. It isn't a steamroller that moves right over you while you lie helpless in front of it. We have more control than that.'

'You've become very philosophical. You must be spending too much time alone. Elliot must be less of a man than I thought he was.'

'Shut up about Elliot!' she shouted, surprising herself as much as she did him. 'Elliot has nothing to do with this! It's about you and me, and no one else!'

He took a step backward from her anger and said too quickly, 'Nothing is that simple. People aren't ever that isolated. Everything we do affects others . . .'

'But what if it didn't?' she interrupted softly, closing the distance between them. She came to a stop within inches of touching him, and lifted her head to look up into his eyes. 'What if nothing existed but you and me, and this place, and this moment. What then?'

Her eyes felt liquid as moisture flooded the corners and threatened to spill over the lids. His face transformed as she watched, the faint lines of tension easing around his mouth. letting the sensuous expressiveness show through. For this instant, what she had proposed had become true. Nothing existed for either of them, but each other. Then his grey eyes lightened as a fleeting thought registered, and she saw the effort of a struggle in the pained lift of his brows.

'If everyone followed that reasoning, the world would go immediately, collectively, mad,' he said huskily, staring into her eyes. 'There would be no honour, no consideration for others, no kindness . . .'

'. . . and no deceit,' she said succinctly, holding his gaze.

'It's a lie,' he whispered desperately, dropping his eyes. 'Pretending like this, that nothing matters but the two of us, that no one else exists—it's a lie.'

'Is it?' Her voice was thin and strained, like a bow string drawn too taut. For to Ruth, at that moment, there *was* nothing else; no one else but this man; no place else on earth but this hill. No world, no people, no past and no future, for either of them. Life had been a series of grey, mindless circumstances, leading inexorably to this one purpose; the only ending that gave all the rest meaning. She had known that feeling once before, on this very spot. Felt this same thundering prelude to a celebration of everything that was right; but he had snatched it from her. This was the second chance, and second chances were rare. There might never be another.

She loved this man. The feeling rolled over her in wave after wave of poignant tenderness as she looked at him. She wanted to huddle with him before a fire on stormy winter evenings; to feel his body wrap around hers in that last, lazy, comfortable embrace before sleep; to face him across a breakfast table in the mornings and touch his tousled hair and watch his eyes lighten to a new day. She wanted hearth, and home, and family; children who squabbled and shattered the deadly quiet of a sleeping house with noisy exuberance; maybe even a dog to scramble across the bed they would share, to wake them together to the unbelievable realisation that the other was still there. But if she could have none of this, and she smiled sadly then, resigned to the certainty that she could not; then at least she could have this one moment, this one time, to last the rest of her life.

She reached out almost shyly, and took his hand in hers. Even in the rapidly descending darkness, she could see the painful question in his eyes. She had said nothing of her thoughts, yet he knew them; and in the narrowing of grey eyes growing suddenly darker, he spoke volumes of love, and need, and despair, and joned her in that small capsule of time where they were the only two people in the world, and this was the only moment that mattered.

She lifted his hand to her lips and kissed the palm that opened to her touch, then he shifted it slightly to cup her face in an indescribably tender gesture. As his hand slid down to encircle the slender column of her neck, her head fell back on her shoulders and she pulled in a quick, audible breath that lifted her breasts towards his hand. When his fingers trailed delicately downward, she dropped her head to meet his eyes, and found them half-closed and flaming with a desire reflected in the strong breathing that flared his nostrils. The skin of his face was tightly drawn against the bones, seeming to pull away until the fire that glowed from his eyes was her only point of reference. She felt the lick of his gaze like a tongue of flame as it coursed over her face, and kept her eyes open to the shifting expressions that altered his features.

His hands were swift and sure as he unfastened the buttons of her dress, but trembled in answer to her shudder when they rested lightly on each breast. She lifted her shoulders as he eased the top of the dress away from her body, then he followed the sleeves with his hands as they slid down the full length of her arms.

She felt the rise of gooseflesh across her chest as the evening breeze danced across her bare skin, then closed her eyes with a tiny gasp when his thumbs brushed across the lacy front of her bra, luring the covered nipples into painful peaks beneath the fabric. She whimpered when he released the front closure of her bra, letting her breasts tumble free into the warm cups of his palms; then moved her own hands with impatient fumbling to release the buttons of his shirt and spread the white panels wide to bare his chest. A silky mat of golden curls twisted in a broad, upside-down triangle that spread across the ripple of smooth muscles, then narrowed to an unseen peak somewhere beneath the band of his trousers. She let her hands float down the highway of tight curls until she felt the muscles just below his ribs jump, with a sharp intake of his breath as counterpoint.

'This is right,' he murmured, his voice trembling, but his eyes steady on hers. 'This is the way it's supposed to be.'

Her hands hesitated at his waist, and she paused to look deeply into his eyes. 'No guilt,' she said shakily, the words both a question and a command.

'No guilt,' he echoed, pulling her against him until her breasts flattened against his chest, blossoming and swelling in response to the caress of the tiny golden hairs against her delicate tissue.

Her dress fluttered to the ground in a gossamer heap of green as he released the sash at her waist, then he eased her away gently and held her by the shoulders. He looked at her for what seemed like a very long time.

She stood shamelessly, proudly, before him, oddly unembarrassed to be examined by a man while she was clad in nothing but a pair of brief panties, even though such a thing had never happened before. She felt the rise of passion suspend itself momentarily on an almost exquisite tide of pleasure, then rise even further as his fingers tightened on her shoulders and his own desire heightened. She saw only the burning lights in his eyes as he cupped her head in both hands; then there was a searing, brief brush of his lips against her mouth, then another, and another, as he touched her lips hesitantly with his then pulled quickly away, again and again until she thought she would cry out with longing. His hands slid down her arms, pinning them to her sides, and frustrated by the immobility, she arched against him while he continued to tease her mouth. He snatched at her lower lips gently with his teeth, lingering long enough to taste the inside tissue with the tip of his tongue before pulling away again. She felt his breath exploding against hers; heard the low, strident moans building in his throat and mingling with the quivering whimpers that escaped her own lips; then he stopped just long enough to show her the dark desire in his eyes before crushing her mouth under his. His hands moved slowly around to her back, then in one fluid movement, he scooped her off the ground and cradled her in gentle, quivering possession against his chest before lowering her carefully to the cool grass. He stripped off the remaining shred of her clothing almost as an afterthought. Then he knelt next to her, leaning back against his heels, making no effort to control the shudder that rippled through his body and made his words come out in short, halting gasps.

'Are you afraid?'

She caught her lower lip between her teeth and stared up at him with wide, trusting eyes. 'Only that you'll leave again,' she said strongly, wondering why she wasn't afraid; why she didn't feel the slightest tremor at giving herself up to an unknown, unfamiliar act with a man she knew could never be hers completely.

He rose slowly to his feet, holding her eyes in the dim light remaining, slid his belt from its holders and let it fall to the ground. When he had discarded his clothes, he lay next to her on the grass, their bodies not touching, tracing delicate patterns from her face to her thighs until she shuddered under his touch and twisted toward him. With his breathing bursting in sharp, ragged gasps, and his chest heaving with the effort of restraint, he pinned her shoulders with his hands and bent to touch the peak of one breast with his tongue, massaging with lips, the tantalising brush of his hair, and the rough caress of his cheek until her back arched upward and his name flew from her throat in an agonised cry. Then she felt his mass hovering over her, the gentle, insistent nudge of thigh against thigh until her legs parted, then the hesitant, cautious thrust against her hips as his body met hers, then entered, and filled her with the throb of passion joining passion until there were no individual bodies left, only the fierce, deafening drumbeat of one heart thundering, one body quivering with pleasure, one voice rising in the vocal confirmation of something that was absolutely, totally right.

Later, when she began to shiver from the chill night air, he gathered her clothes and began to dress her with the gentle solicitude one would show to a child. His brows nearly touched as he struggled with the intracies of her bra, and his lips pursed in concentration, and he looked amazingly young and innocent in the light of a pale rising moon.

She smiled, aching with tenderness, and brushed his hair aside with an almost maternal gesture. His eyes stopped on hers, and for the moment, there was no sadness in them.

'So you never loved Martin,' he said quietly. 'Not like this.'

'I loved Martin like a father,' she smiled, 'or like a grandfather. He was eighty-three, Hampton.'

'Oh,' he said sheepishly; and then, as if he had just remembered something, 'Elliot isn't eighty-three, and he loves you, you know.'

'And he knows I love you,' she said simply. 'It's why he left tonight, I think. But I don't want to talk about other people. Not yet.'

She pulled his head to her lips, silencing him with a lingering kiss. He mustn't talk. Not about Elliot, or Martin, or anyone. It would bring the outside world up on to the hill, with all its obligations and its bleak future.

He pulled away gently and searched her eyes. 'We can't hide from it, Ruth. We have to talk about it.'

She dropped her head and shook it miserably from side to side. 'There's nothing to say. Talking won't change anything.'

'Ruth!' he said sharply, cradling her head in his

hands and forcing her to look up at him. 'We've already changed everything! Surely you don't think we can go on as if tonight never happened!'

She nodded wordlessly as one tear trembled at the corner of her eye.

'I can't!' he whispered urgently, pulling her against his chest. 'I can't do it. Not now. I can't marry her.'

She pushed away abruptly and looked at him in desperation. 'But you have to!'

He shook his head with a small smile. 'You were right in the beginning. We belong together. Pretending we don't isn't fair to any of us; Christie especially.'

'No, no,' Ruth whispered, horrified by a victory she once would have given years of her life to attain. 'I didn't know then, I didn't understand. You have no choice but to marry her. I knew that before tonight, I knew before we made love that it wouldn't change anything, and it didn't matter. I still wanted us to have . . . this. But nothing has changed.'

'Nothing has changed!' He grabbed her shoulders and shook her lightly, trying to contain his frustration. 'Of course it has! My God, Ruth, this is right. What we feel for each other is right, and anything that prevents it is wrong! Stop thinking of Christie, and think of us!'

'I am,' she said flatly, pushing away and reaching for her dress. 'That's the only thing I ever think of.'

The magic was gone now, and the air was suddenly unbearably cold. She slipped her arms into the sleeves of her dress with the tired motions of a much older woman. 'It wouldn't work, Hampton,' she said dispiritedly. 'Not with a man like you. You'd carry your guilt about Christie with you forever, and eventually, it would destroy any chance of happiness we had.'

The light faded from his eyes as she spoke, as if he were just awakening from a wonderful dream, realising that it had only been a dream, after all. Her words only echoed something he had known all along: that his past had trapped him, and that there was no way out. This had been his last grasp for happiness. The last, desperate reach of a man who knows the effort is pointless, but who must try anyway.

'So what's left for us?' he asked dully, not really expecting an answer.

'Friendship?' she whispered in a soft plea.

His laugh was totally unexpected, mirthless, and somehow frightening.

Ruth occupied herself with a nervous straightening of her clothes while he dressed, waiting for the horrible, bitter laughter to fade away.

'You can do this, then?' he asked finally as they both stood facing one another. There was a chilling, demanding edge to his voice. 'You can walk away from tonight, and forget it?'

'I never expected it to make any difference,' she said softly. 'I knew we might have just this one time, and nothing more. It was more than I hoped for.'

The earnestness of her moist gaze and the despairing tremble in her voice escaped him. He only heard the words. 'Just this one time,' he repeated tonelessly. 'That's what it was? The proverbial one-night stand?' He shook his head in the self-deprecating gesture of one who can hardly believe his own foolishness, and muttered under his breath. 'And to think I was the one worried about diminishing our relationship with casual sex! And all the while that's what you wanted! That's totally backwards, isn't it? Isn't it the woman who's supposed to demand commitment before sex, and the man who's supposed to shrug it all off?'

She could hardly believe what she was hearing, and the words of protest died in her throat. He had jumped to the conclusion so quickly that she could not react in time to stop him. His face looked white and pinched in the pale moonlight, and for an instant, before his features hardened to stone, she caught a glimpse of an expression that was openly wounded. He thought she had used him. The realisation astounded her, and she shook her head in mute surprise, trying to gather her scattered thoughts.

'Tell me,' he interrupted her astonished silence, 'how does a woman like you select the man she'll use for her first experience? I'd be interested to know. Why me? Why not Elliot, for instance?'

She shuddered under the insult and took a quick step backward, away from his glowering contempt. The sudden attack had shocked her into silence—it seemed ridiculous to even have to bother to deny such a preposterous accusation—and in that moment of hesitation, before she instinctively jumped to her own defence, proclaiming her love and the importance of this night, she realised that such an act would only make the future harder for both of them.

Let him believe she had used him. Let him think that to her, this night had only been a casual, one-time affair. Better that, than to go through life tied to another woman, knowing that love was always just beyond his reach. If he thought the love was not there, had never been there, he would suffer less. It was the only thing left she could do for him.

Her lips were still parted in the circle of surprise. She had to concentrate fiercely to bring her features into rigid expressionlessness; a mask that would convince him his suspicions had been right.

There was a brief flash of pain as he watched the transformation, then his lips curved in a cynical half-smile. She had not denied his accusations, and her silence was an admission of guilt.

'I certainly hope your first experience lived up to all your expectations,' he said sarcastically, then he laughed bitterly. 'The tender first love! That first, touching time one remembers fondly, but never takes too seriously! I suppose I should feel flattered that you chose me for such a momentous honour. You'll forgive me, but I can't quite manage that.'

A note of despair crept through the contempt, and Ruth had to clench her fists at her sides to keep from reaching out for him. He was leaving the door open, keeping the conversation going; standing there, staring down at her, giving her one last chance to speak out and deny it all. Keeping silent was the hardest thing she had ever done in her life.

She tried not to notice the moonlight glimmering weakly in his hair, seeping into the white of his shirt, making it glow against the deep tan of his throat. She tried not to focus on the two deep, unfathomable shadows where his eyes were, knowing she could not bear the contempt if she saw it too clearly. But his silence was too long; too final. The words were clambering up her throat in an effort to get out, and she couldn't hold them in much longer.

'Fine,' he said finally, and the word snapped and spat like the edge of a whip severing the last thin thread that held them together. Then without warning, he seized her roughly by the sides of her head and crushed his lips against hers. The act was more one of desperation than of caring, and for some reason, it made her want to cry. He released her just as quickly with a disdainful, dismissive shove, and she had to blink hard to hold back the tears.

'By the way,' he said with a sardonic lift of his brows. His defences were fully in place now, and his words were coldly indifferent. 'I almost forgot what I originally intended to do tonight. I wanted to apologise, for my behaviour that night at the club.'

'There's no need for that,' she said quickly, wondering at the tiny, broken sound of her voice.

'Indeed there is,' he interrupted harshly. 'I behaved like a jealous schoolboy—that's almost laughable now, isn't it? And obviously, I had no right to those feelings. No right at all.'

She wanted to scream at him, to grab him by the shoulders and shake him until the strength left her body. If he had no right to those feelings, who did? By denying them, he denied everything that existed between them; eliminated it once and for all, shoved it away in a tiny, dark drawer somewhere as a mistake that had to be hidden from sight.

She forced herself to look at him steadily, and said nothing.

'That's what I thought,' he said flatly, as if her silence had answered yet another question. 'So to continue with my apology, your relationship with Elliot, or with any other man, for that matter, is none of my business. I was labouring under a ridiculous, fairytale delusion at the time, you see. I promise you it won't happen again.'

She walked a few paces behind him towards the car, and only when they were both settled inside with the engine running did she turn to face him. 'Are you giving me your blessing then?' she asked quietly. 'Go ahead, Ruth, take Elliot, don't let me stand in your way. That sort of thing?'

He shifted into gear without even looking at her. 'You could say that, I suppose; although the blessing isn't really mine to give, is it? Whatever you choose to do with your body, or your life, is no concern of mine.'

She faced front slowly, feeling the life drain out of her. It was over, then. It was finally over. He had just given her away.

They made the drive home in total silence, and when Hampton eased the car to a stop in front of her building, she got out quickly, without a single word of farewell. She heard the tyres spit gravel behind her as the car sped away.

Elliot looked up from his hunched posture at the kitchen table when she came in. She saw concern and doubt in the lift of his brows, and managed a weak little smile.

He straightened slowly to his full height, tossing his head to throw his hair back from his face. Ruth could sense his impulse to comfort her as if it had been spoken aloud.

'I'm all right, Elliot,' she reassured him softly.
'Really.'

There was a subtle shift in their relationship that
Ruth could feel across the room. By leaving her with
Hampton, Elliot had acknowledged the special bond
between the two, and his own inability to diminish it. It
may even have surprised him, Ruth thought, to realise
that his own feelings hadn't been as strong as he
thought.

He was her friend, this man; and perhaps that was all
he was ever meant to be. His love was genuine enough,
it just wasn't the kind that moved mountains, shook the
earth under your feet, or left you dying when it went
away.

There was concern in his eyes, and comfort in the
arms that finally pulled her close; but it was a brotherly
embrace, perhaps even a fatherly one; and they both
realised that at the same moment. They relaxed in each
other's arms then, content to have found the limits of
their relationship; completely comfortable in the roles
they were meant to play all along.

CHAPTER EIGHT

HAMPTON was at the house the next morning, striding through the rooms with a long-legged purposeful gait, approving the progress he saw with an occasional nod. Sam accompanied him at Ruth's insistence, while she remained in the library alone, pleading the need to alter one of the drawings.

'Funny, you don't look all that busy.' He appeared suddenly in the doorway, startling her as she stood idly looking out the window.

She turned quickly to face him, an excuse ready on her lips, but let it die unspoken when her eyes met his. There was a cold, frank appraisal in the steady gaze he levelled at her; one that made her feel suddenly cheap, like goods on a shelf. She shrugged lightly to hide the shudder, and walked casually over to the drawing boards.

He hesitated in the doorway, as if trying to decide whether to enter the room or leave. He finally compromised by leaning against the frame with his arms folded across his chest. His light hair was dulled with a dusting of cement powder, and there was a grey smudge across one cheek.

'So how does it feel to be a fallen woman?' he asked snidely, acknowledging the flash of anger in her eyes with the slight lift of his brows. 'Sorry,' he said sarcastically. 'That's a bit archaic for this day and age, isn't it? Women don't fall from grace any more, they just become experienced.'

She had less trouble controlling her anger than her despair, but revealed neither in the stony set of her features, although her cheeks were flushed a violent red.

'Amazing that you can still blush,' he said flippantly.

129

'I would have thought that sort of thing was well behind you now.'

From any other man, the undeserved insults would have met a violent, righteous rage. From Hampton, they prompted only a sick, clinging despair it took all her willpower to conceal. Her lack of reaction surprised him, and he acknowledged her control with a slight nod. His gaze was insultingly familiar as it wandered over her baggy coveralls before returning to her face.

'I liked the green dress you were wearing last night,' he said. 'It picked up the colour of your eyes.'

There was an underlying sincerity to the remark that caught her off-guard, and she dropped her eyes quickly so he would not see her uncertainty.

He walked into the room, strolling past the design boards with an almost casual aloofness, brushing past her as if she weren't there. 'You're ahead of schedule here, aren't you?'

'Yes,' she answered cautiously, hating this awkward, stilted conversation, but helpless to stop it. 'The crews have been exceptional. The house should be finished by September.'

He shrugged indifferently. 'No need to rush. We won't need it before October.'

He turned towards her slowly, leaning back against the library table, crossing his legs at the ankle. His expression was dispassionately cool, his manner perfectly controlled, and his smile had a sly quality she had never seen before.

'It's obvious that I'm making you very uncomfortable,' he said unexpectedly. 'I'd like to know why.'

'That's a stupid question!' she snapped without thinking.

'Don't tell me you're feeling a touch of remorse? Just a shade of conscience?'

'No,' she answered immediately. 'None whatsoever.'

'That's what I thought. In that case, since you have

no aversion to intimacy without commitment, perhaps we'll do it again sometime. I'm finding that shedding ideals is a great deal easier than acquiring them. If I work at it long enough, perhaps I'll become as coldly practical as you are. It's something to aim for, isn't it?'

He walked past her on his way to the door, intentionally brushing her breasts with a casual lift of one hand. It was an insolent, demeaning gesture, and Ruth gasped at the extent of his contempt.

He mistook the sound for one of passion, and paused to look at her with brows arched over cold grey eyes. 'My, my. You're easily aroused, aren't you? I can hardly believe that . . .'

'Hampton! Stop it!' she shouted, flipping off the cap that contained her hair and tossing it on the table. Thick waves of shocking red tumbled down over her shoulders, and Hampton winced at the sight as if it had wounded him somehow.

'What should I stop?' he asked quickly, his eyes narrow and intense.

'Stop . . . treating me like this,' she answered lamely, knowing she could say nothing more than that.

His smile was bitter, but controlled. 'And how would you like me to treat you?'

The words left her mouth in a rush, and she closed her eyes against the pain of saying them. 'As if last night never happened.'

She heard his footsteps as he walked away, and opened her eyes in time to see him turn at the doorway.

'You ask entirely too much,' he said flatly, and then he was gone.

She collapsed into the nearest chair, and noted with almost absent surprise that her hands were shaking uncontrollably.

'What's bothering you, Ruth?' Elliot asked later that night as they worked over the Summit sketches.

'What makes you think something's bothering me?' she asked testily.

He nodded towards the drawing she was holding. 'You just erased the support wall for the entire second floor. If you wanted a rambler, why didn't you say so?'

'Oh, damn,' she muttered, crumpling the drawing in one hand.

He ruffled her hair affectionately and bent to kiss her cheek. 'Come on. Talk about it, whatever it is.'

She got up from her seat and paced in frustrated agitation. 'I saw Hampton today,' she blurted out finally.

'Oh.'

She shot him a warning glance. 'You say that like it explains everything.'

He gave her a knowing smile. 'Doesn't it?'

She sighed hard once and went on with her pacing. 'I did a fine, stupid, noble thing, Elliot. I let him believe that there was nothing between us; that I was just using him.'

'Well, stupid was certainly the right adjective. Why would you do a silly thing like that?'

'I thought it would be easier,' she said tonelessly, 'easier for him, if he thought I didn't love him.'

Elliot sighed in exasperation. 'And I suppose noble was the right adjective, too. But then I always thought nobility and stupidity were usualy one and the same. Don't tell me he bought it. The man can't be that blind!'

'Oh, he bought it all right,' Ruth said miserably, 'and you could cut his contempt with a knife. I don't think I can stand it, Elliot. I don't think I can see him again.'

He moved quickly to lift her chin with one hand. 'Now listen to me,' he said sternly. 'No matter what games you two insist on playing, Hampton is giving you the start you need to set your career soaring. You can't give that up, and if you refuse to see him again, that's exactly what you'll be doing.' He pulled her into his arms and she let herself sag against him. 'Besides,' he said into her hair, 'you'll have to see him again. Christie called today, inviting us both out to dinner tomorrow night. And I already accepted.'

Ruth stiffened instantly in his arms and jerked her head back to glare at him. 'Why did you do that? You had no right to accept for me, especially knowing what you know!'

He shook his head with a gentle smile. 'It's what *you* don't know that worries me. You and Hampton. You're tearing each other apart for the sake of a woman who doesn't give a damn about either one of you. And that's the biggest reason that we're going to that dinner. Maybe we'll get lucky and Christie will show her true colours.'

Ruth narrowed her eyes in exasperation. 'Oh, Elliot. Don't start that again. You really hate her, don't you?'

'Not at all,' he said artlessly. 'Not any more than I hate cobras, or tornadoes, or anything else that's deadly. I just don't trust her, that's all. But don't worry your head about my paranoia. Just think of this dinner as practice. Practice at being cool with Hampton, so at least you two can work together. I'll be there to help you get through it, and if you can manage tomorrow night, maybe you can manage working with him after all. And that's what's important now, isn't it? With or without Hampton, your work will still be there.'

She stared soundlessly at the wall behind his head until her vision blurred, then nodded once.

The foursome that met for dinner at the Meridian Room the following evening was a painfully awkward group. Ruth tried to recapture the warmth of the intangible bond that she and Hampton and Elliot had shared, but it seemed like something that had happened a million years ago, to different people entirely.

She greeted Christie with a pretence of pleasure, wondering if her words rang as falsely to others as they did in her own ears. As always, Christie was the picture of striking vitality. The high natural colouring in her cheeks, the glowing complexion, the bright eyes—all were hallmarks of a healthy, well-conditioned athlete, yet she maintained them remarkably without ever leaving the confines of a wheelchair.

The moment she saw the darker woman's daring, ice-blue gown, the perfection of mounded curls that framed her face and lifted to a dark, glossy crown, Ruth regretted not taking more trouble with her own appearance. Elliot had even made a timid suggestion that she wear some jewellery, or wear her hair up in a more elegant style. She had refused flatly, bristling at the intimation that she was in some way trying to compete with Christie's feminine allure. Aside from the fact that she never thought of herself as Christie's rival, she was simply unpractised at packaging herself like goods on display, and found the whole idea totally abhorrent.

But now, with Hampton's eyes on her with apparent indifference, she almost wished she had mustered the effort. If nothing else, it would have been satisfying to see a flicker of desire in the cool grey eyes.

Her dress was flat black and starkly simple, with long tight sleeves and a high neckline. She wore her long hair loose and free, and the golden highlights dancing in the full red waves provided the only colour in an otherwise drab presentation. She felt herself pale into the background of Christie's vibrant, colourful appearance especially when Hampton appraised her coolly, then immediately shifted his eyes back to his fiancée.

Elliot was darkly dashing, as usual, and without Hampton for comparison, would easily have been the most desirable man in the room. But Hampton was effortlessly elegant, wearing a light spring suit with an almost incidental grace, making Elliot's brooding handsomeness look brash and somewhat unpolished.

Of the four of them, Christie alone seemed genuinely

delighted to be there, anticipating a gay evening with friends. 'Isn't this lovely?' she remarked happily after cocktails were served. 'There aren't three other people in the world I'd rather be with tonight.'

The comment made Ruth feel guilty for not enjoying herself, and she determined to make a strong effort for the sake of this innocent woman, who had no inkling of the pain her very existence had caused.

'Really?' Elliot countered, directing a politely quizzical expression at Christie. 'Now why is that?'

Ruth nudged him furiously under the table with her knee while her face remained frozen in an artificial smile.

Christie never batted a beautiful blue eye, however, and apparently discerned no ulterior motive from the blatant question. 'Because you're all beautiful people,' she replied with a sweet smile. 'Inside and out, every one of you! And you all fit so well together, have you noticed that? You, Ruth and Tray—you all seem to have this common thread that pulls you together somehow. It almost makes me feel like an outsider.'

Her ingenuous remark was so without envy, and so perilously close to Ruth's own perception of the relationship that the three of them shared, that she was genuinely taken aback. Somehow she had thought of Christie as an oblivious child, not terribly aware of the nuances of other people's relationships. But if she was astute enough to see this, perhaps Ruth's feelings for Hampton were equally apparent. She felt immediately guilty, almost as if she had been caught at some wrongdoing by an innocent victim, and would at any moment be publicly accused.

She scavenged in her thoughts for a subject to steer the conversation in another direction. 'Are the plans for the wedding well underway, Christie?' she asked with what she hoped would be construed as idle interest. As soon as the words were out of her mouth, she cringed from the answer. It was the first thing that had popped into her mind, and the last subject she wanted to discuss.

'Oh, I wouldn't know about that. The family is handling the details, and I haven't interfered. I do hate the fuss and bother of such affairs. Besides, it's going to be very awkward. Tray hasn't seen my parents for years, and I think both sides were quite content with that arrangement.' She patted Hampton's hand and flashed him a consoling smile. 'And to let the cat out of the bag, as they say, that's the real reason I begged for this dinner tonight. Tray was adamant about being too busy for a social evening, but I insisted.'

Ruth met Hampton's eyes directly for the first time, but found them veiled and unreadable. So he hadn't relished the idea of this stilted gathering either, she thought. That was some comfort, at least.

'The truth of it is,' Christie continued, leaning forward across the table with an expectant, con-spiratorial smile, 'that I've decided we should skip the wedding!'

Ruth's heart was off and thundering uncontrollably before Christie could finish her thought.

'At least *that* wedding,' Christie amended with a secretive smile. 'I'd rather have a small ceremony here, and avoid that hideous traditional pomp and publicity; and I want you two to be our only witnesses.'

She leaned back with a smug, delighted smile, obviously pleased with her announcement.

It was an obvious surprise to Hampton, and although his expression was tightly controlled, his frown of disbelief was genuine. 'I had no idea you were considering such a thing,' he said quietly.

'Oh, Tray,' she bubbled, 'I do hate to disillusion you, but in spite of the fact that you've known me most of my life, I think you'll learn in time that I still have the ability to surprise you every now and then. That's what keeps a relationship interesting, don't you think?' She directed this last question to Elliot, who was frowning in earnest concentration all out of proportion to the conversation.

'Sometimes,' he replied carefully. 'And sometimes it's just plain scary.'

She laughed, almost brittly, Ruth thought, and raised her glass to Hampton. 'Well, what do you think, darling? Do you approve of my little scheme to deprive family and public of their little three-ring circus? I know how much you hate spectacles, and I was sure you'd be pleased.'

'Whatever you prefer, Christie,' he said solemnly.

She leaned sideways to plant a dry kiss on his cheek. 'Good! We agree, then. And you . . .' she nodded at Ruth and Elliot, '. . . I hope you'll consent to be our witnesses. I know it will mean a great deal to Tray if his two very best friends . . . in fact, they're your only friends, aren't they, darling? . . . anyway, if you could be there, it would be absolutely perfect.'

It would be absolutely perfect. The words echoed and re-echoed in Ruth's battered mind, and she wondered if this was how people felt when sanity started to slip away. You're sitting here, she told herself, opposite a beautiful, innocent, crippled woman, who has just asked two people whose friendship she values to witness the most joyous occasion of her life. And what of those two people? One of them loves her husband-to-be beyond all reason, has slept with her husband-to-be; and the other thinks she is the reincarnation of the wicked witch of the west. Beyond that, the husband-to-be thinks the bridesmaid-to-be is only slightly better than a common whore, yet we all sit here smiling, perpetrating the most preposterous hypocrisy of all time.

Ruth was unaware of the stiff, frozen smile she wore, or the glazed appearance of eyes gone suddenly blank. Elliot's hand squeezing insistently at her knee under the table brought her to attention in time to witness one of his rare, brilliant smiles. It was directed at Christie, but it seemed to light up the entire table. 'I, for one, wouldn't miss it for the world,' he said smoothly, inclining his head in a gallant nod that left a thatch of glossy black hair angled charmingly across his forehead.

Christie stared at him for a moment, her lips parted slightly, as bewitched by the smile as any woman would have been. At his worst, Elliot was mysteriously intriguing, at his best, as he was now, he was absolutely irresistible.

'Wonderful,' she said softly, pulling her eyes away reluctantly and brandishing her empty glass towards Hampton. 'I think I'll have another,' she said lightly. 'And you should too, darling, because what all this means is that we can be married much sooner. Now that's cause for celebration, isn't it?'

There was absolutely no change in Hampton's expression, which was the true measure of how deeply Christie's words had affected him. Ruth tried to look away, tried to shift her gaze anywhere else but at Hampton's eyes; but he caught her glance and held it with his own. She steeled herself against the expected contempt, and was surprised not to see it. His eyes were empty and flat, and somehow that was worse.

Elliot broke the silence that was lingering too long with a softly spoken question that sounded like an explosion to Ruth. 'Have you chosen a date, Christie?'

His words broke the spell, and though Ruth's and Hampton's expressons remained tightly controlled, they both shifted their eyes to Christie.

'How about July the fourth?' she suggested with a coy glance at Hampton. 'Can you fit a wedding into that busy schedule of yours on such short notice, Tray? That's only a month from tomorrow.'

'Don't be silly!' he snapped with uncharacteristic harshness. 'Our wedding will take precedence over everything. Just as it always has.'

It was the first time Ruth had heard him address Christie with anything but the utmost solicitude, and although she cringed from the obvious impatience in his tone, Christie rebounded without a tremor.

'Of course it has, darling. I was only teasing. Now that that's settled, perhaps we can have some champagne. The occasion would certainly seem to merit it, don't you think?'

Thank God for Elliot, Ruth thought as the evening wore on. He was carrying off the insane façade of a friendly celebration all on his own. There was no way she could even pretend to participate, and she let her first glass of champagne go flat and barely tasted while the others finished one bottle and went on to the second.

Christie's giddy banter with the waiter who finally took their food order made it all too apparent that she had had far too much to drink. Her repeated efforts to pronounce the French entrée finally dissolved into giggles, and Hampton completed her request for her with a disapproving glare.

'Perhaps we should make it an early evening,' he said sternly, moving to rise from his chair.

'Oh, no,' Christie slurred, shaking her head so vehemently that a lone, springy curl dislodged to dangle crazily over her forehead.

The old nursery rhyme popped unbidden into Ruth's thoughts. 'There was a little girl, who had a little curl, right in the middle of her forehead. And when she was good, she was very, very good; but when she was bad, she was . . .'

'No, no, no,' Christie continued. 'I'll have a little air, then I'll be ju-u-st fine. Besides, I'm having such a *good* time, Tray. Don't be cross, please?'

She could barely enunciate her consonants, but the innocent, childlike pout was so appealing, her expression so plaintive, that Ruth felt a twinge of sympathy. She looked less like a drunken woman than a somewhat naughty, contrite child.

'It is a celebration, after all,' Elliot put in gallantly. 'Ease up a little, Hampton. I'll just take Christie out on the terrace for a while before the first course arrives.'

Hampton's face darkened dangerously at Elliot's interference, but Christie's reaction was immediate, forestalling anything he might have said.

'Elliot, you're a gentleman, and a darling,' she cooed, leaning over to place a hand high on his thigh. She chattered on while Elliot shot to rigid, surprised attention under the hand's unexpected, warm pressure. It was obvious to Ruth that Christie was blissfully unaware of the reaction her gesture had caused, and almost laughed aloud at Elliot's discomfiture. Still, it was just as well that the table blocked the drunken comedy of errors from Hampton's view.

Elliot rose quickly and whisked Christie towards the terrace doors with a parting, mysterious wink at Ruth. If he thought he was doing her a favour by leaving her alone with Hampton, he was wrong. The atmosphere was instantly fraught with tension.

'Sorry about that,' Hampton said sullenly, wincing when the sound of Christie's laughter came floating in from the distant terrace. 'In fact I'm sorry about the entire evening. I had no idea . . .'

'Never mind,' Ruth said quickly, concentrating furiously on the intricacies of her crystal water goblet. 'Only . . .' she raised eyes suddenly moist to meet his squarely.

'Only what?' he asked gently, his expression softer than it had been all evening.

'Never mind.' She shook her head slightly, unwilling for the moment to force the issue of his remoteness. She bent her head and stared blindly at the napkin on her lap.

'That's a striking dress,' he said unexpectedly, and she lifted her head, feeling colour spring to her cheeks.

'Elliot thought it was much too drab,' she said carefully, trying to sound casual. 'Up until the moment we left, he was trying to force jewellery on me.'

'Elliot was wrong,' he said, his eyes directly on her. 'Some women don't need ornamentation. You're one of them.'

Her flush deepened, and she looked down. He shouldn't do that, she thought. If he's going to be indifferent, he should be completely indifferent, and not make personal observations. Otherwise, this is never going to work. I'll just keep fighting it.

'Hampton,' she blurted suddenly, unable to control herself, 'you can't get married next month.'

His features froze instantly. Within the space of a second, all trace of warmth was gone. 'Oh? Why not?'

She stammered under the icy glare. 'Because ... because the house won't be finished,' she said in a rush. 'The downstairs work has hardly begun, and the upstairs hasn't been started. You couldn't possibly live there with all that work going on, and it's going to take months yet!' She was almost babbling, unconscious of precisely what she was saying, knowing only that she had to keep talking before he silenced her once and for all. 'You'd have no privacy at all, for one thing, with all the workmen there; and there isn't a single room we can finish in time. You wouldn't have guestrooms, or a kitchen, or children's rooms ...' Suddenly her own words penetrated the confusion of her thoughts, and the sentence trailed off in a sick, sinking mire of what she had said aloud, but never really considered.

She stared straight ahead, unseeing, her lips still open in the shape that formed her last word. Of course they would sleep together, she chided herself. Why had she never thought of that? How stupid she had been! That's what marriage was all about, after all. You sleep together, you have children; and even if there was nothing there to start with, the children bind you together in a common purpose, and outsiders never share that. It's the one tie that can't be broken. So there would be little Hamptons, little Christies, and eventually, they would be a family. Christie would be a wonderful mother, and a devoted wife, and even if Hampton never felt again the shattering, roaring moments of passion they had shared, he would learn to be content.

Her eyes focused gradually as the scenario subsided in her mind, and she saw Hampton looking at her strangely.

'It seems incredible,' he said a little shakily, 'but you really don't know, do you?'

'I don't know what?' she asked dully.

He pursed his lips and frowned, then spoke in a low, steady voice. 'Christie is paralysed, Ruth. You knew that.'

'Yes, I know. Her legs.'

'No. Not just her legs. From the waist down.' His words were clipped. 'There will be no children. No physical relations at all. She's incapable of it.'

When her eyes began to smart from dryness, she blinked. What he was saying was absolutely unthinkable. No man would knowingly commit himself to a celibate future, and no woman would expect such a sacrifice. Unless the man was Hampton, she realised suddenly; tormented by guilt, trapped by an inflexible code of honour. And even if his passionate nature forced him into occasional, tawdry liaisons with women who would temporarily assuage his physical needs, with each such encounter, the guilt would increase, and the jaws of the circular trap would close even more tightly. His life would become an agonised battleground of his own vibrant, sensual nature pitted against his rigid standards of behaviour. He would want desperately to honour his marriage vows, as he honoured his word whenever it was given; but he would be doomed to failure, and for a man like Hampton, failure was unacceptable.

'You really didn't know, did you?' His voice prodded gently at her consciousness, and she forced herself up from the depths of her thoughts to face him squarely.

'You can't do it, Hampton,' she whispered intently. 'You can't go through with it.'

His eyes flickered briefly, then he remarked, 'I think we've been over this ground before. I can do it, and I will. I pay my debts.'

There was something dreadfully, horribly off-key about the whole situation. Christie didn't know Hampton well enough. She couldn't, or she would realise this pathetic sham of a marriage would destroy him. Innocent, crippled, reaching for the shards of fulfilment in a life brutally altered; she probably assumed Hampton would find physical satisfaction outside the marriage, and did not begrudge him that. But even if she could live with such an arrangement, Ruth knew that Hampton could not.

With a flash of insight that left her stunned, it occurred to Ruth that the destruction of the man she loved was imminent, and that it couldn't have been more completely devastating had it been planned, step by careful step. How sad Christie, through naïveté or ignorance, or both, was the unwitting instrument in a long, ugly series of circumstances that would destroy the man they both loved.

Part of her wanted to explain it to Christie, to make her see what her innocent quest for happiness would cost; but she knew that by doing that, she would sever completely the strained, ragged thread still holding Hampton to her. He had made his choices with his eyes open, and there were no options left.

When she could force her eyes to meet his again, she found them narrowed with a smile of cynical resignation. For the moment, the subject was closed.

Christie was strangely subdued when Elliot finally wheeled her back to the table. Two high spots of colour rode her cheeks, making her look strangely like an over-painted doll. Elliot was very nearly bursting with a smug glee as he pushed her from behind; an expression that vanished instantly when he resumed his place at the table. Ruth puzzled at his inexplicable high spirits, and at the fact that he was obviously taking great care that neither Christie nor Hampton should be aware of them, but put it off to his whimsical moods. Oddly enough, he was tenderly solicitous towards Christie during the meal, and Ruth stifled a growing irritation with his abrupt and obvious change of heart. He had been Christie's worst critic before the evening, but she had certainly charmed him into the role of an infatuated admirer. It seemed that at last Elliot had seen Christie for exactly what she was, and the reality enchanted him. At least Ruth would be spared the frustration of defending her character in the future against Elliot's suspicions.

By unspoken mutal consent, the party dispersed immediately after the meal. Christie had fluttered flirtatiously under Elliot's attention for a time, but had gradually sobered with the ingestion of food, and all pretence of frivolous gaiety faded away. She was quietly thoughtful when they parted, and her gaze lingered briefly on Ruth with an expression that would have seemed calculating on a less innocent face.

'Thank you for coming, Ruth,' she said simply, pressing her hand. She nodded once to Elliot, then Hampton wheeled her away without a word of farewell to either of them.

Elliot smiled silently all the way home, piloting the car with a gay recklessness that was particularly irritating to Ruth's morose frame of mind. 'What are you so damn happy about?' she snapped finally, but Elliot didn't answer. He merely reached over and patted her knee absently, in the manner of an adult casually mollifying a child.

CHAPTER NINE

RUTH woke with a blistering headache the next morning, as if somehow she had been burdened with the hangover from Christie's overindulgence. She pulled on a robe and stumbled out to the kitchen, where Elliot was happily busy at the stove, whistling while he worked.

'Please, Elliot,' she begged wincing at the shrill sound. 'I think I have Christie's headache.'

He chuckled softly at that, not even bothering to suppress his amusement. 'Sometimes, Ruth, you say the most astonishingly perceptive things. Here. Eggs Benedict as you've never had them.'

She didn't have a hangover. That was certain. The dish he set before her was a visual and aromatic enticement that almost dispelled her headache entirely, and she lifted her fork before he had time to serve himself.

'Glad to see you have an appetite,' he commented with a wry grin. 'From your mood last night, I wasn't certain you'd ever find the heart to eat again.'

'There was better reason for my mood than you know, Elliot,' she replied glumly, and proceeded to tell him everything she had learned and surmised from her brief conversation with Hampton.

Elliot listened politely until she had finished, and frowned. His face darkened further with every passing second of silence, and a vein at the side of his forehead pulsed visibly. When he finally spoke, his words exploded softly with the quivering intensity that comes from suppressing the impulse to shout. 'Do you understand now? Can you begin to see it at last?'

'See what?'

145

He took a tremendous breath and held it behind tightly closed lips, then released it slowly. 'You think Christie is self-sacrificing? Who will be sacrificed in a marriage like that?' he shouted. 'Christie? Or Hampton?'

'I know that, Elliot,' she said softly. 'Better than you. But I don't think Christie really understands it. She couldn't, or . . .'

He interrupted her with a violent expletive. 'Don't be so naïve, Ruth! She may look like an empty-headed seventeen-year-old, but she isn't! She's an adult, intelligent woman who knows exactly what she's doing! I'm not sure what she's after, but the by-product is going to be Hampton's destruction, unless she's stopped!'

There was a sickening, final quality about the silence that followed his outburst. Ruth was almost relieved when the door buzzer startled them both, and jumped up quickly to answer it.

'Sally. Hello. Come in, please.'

Sally stood in the hall, one hand resting on a trim, jean-clad hip; the other dangling a blank cheque in front of Ruth's nose. 'You haven't been to the office in over a week,' she scolded. 'And your one and only slave is getting restless. So is her landlord. Rent's due today.'

'Oh, Sally, I'm sorry. I missed payday, didn't I? Come on in. I'll make it out right now.'

It was first time Sally had ever been in Ruth's apartment, so she looked around in idle curiosity as Ruth led her into the kitchen. 'We've had two serious enquiries about design work this week, Ruth, and I'll make sure they don't find out where you live. This is absolutely the worst example of interior design I've ever . . .' Her mouth dropped open and she stopped dead when she saw Elliot rising from the kitchen table. 'Oh. Sorry. I didn't know you . . .' She shrugged and rolled big brown eyes in mute embarassment.

'It's not what you think, Sally,' Ruth laughed, knowing the denial would sound feeble with her standing there in her housecoat.

Sally looked Elliot up and down in a frank appraisal, her brows raised sceptically. 'If that's the truth, then you're crazier than I thought you were. You've got a specimen like this in your apartment for breakfast, and you aren't claiming ownership?'

'We keep trying to fall in love,' Ruth smiled, 'but it just doesn't work out. We're friends, Sally. That's all.'

'Well then!' Sally levelled a hard look at Elliot, then straightened to her full height and addressed him solemnly. 'I am twenty-four years old, in excellent health, have all my own teeth, and could give you many sons.'

Ruth laughed out loud, but Elliot merely grinned, his eyes glinting with mischief. 'I'd have to see the teeth,' he said, pulling a poker face.

'Anytime.'

'Don't mind her, Elliot,' Ruth put in. 'She's always playing hard to get.'

Elliot laughed and silenced Sally's protests when he offered breakfast by pushing her forcibly into a chair. She followed his movements in the kitchen with a look of exaggerated adoration, her chin resting in one hand.

'He cooks, too?' she asked with wonder.

'Wait 'till you taste,' Ruth smiled.

There was a bittersweet edge to the satisfaction Ruth felt as she watched Elliot and Sally relate over the meal. She had a vague sensation of puzzle pieces rushing to fit together, as if the three of them were part of a whole that was somehow incomplete. Worse than that, listening to the casual conversation that barely concealed the immediate attraction between the two reminded her of her first meeting with Hampton. There was envy that a similar feeling should exist between two other people, and that nothing stood in their way.

Elliot was more animated than Ruth had ever seen

him, filling Sally in on the details of The Summit, and when that subject was exhausted, rambling on in answer to Sally's coaxing questions about his childhood and college years. Ruth listened quietly to stories she had never heard, her brows arched slightly in amused surprise. Sally had learned more about Elliot Shore in twenty minutes than she had learned in as many days.

Elliot stopped suddenly in mid-sentence, frowning in pleased bewilderment. 'Listen to me! I'm baring my soul like a garrulous old woman, and believe me, that's totally out of character. Tell her, Ruth. I'm really a quiet, secretive, mysterious man.'

He looked innocently boyish and slightly abashed at that moment, and Ruth felt the sudden thrust of maturity, as if she were witnessing the naïve impetuousness of a younger brother. 'Sally turns every conversation into a confessional,' she smiled. 'That's her speciality. Give her five minutes, and she'll know everything about you worth knowing, and what you don't tell voluntarily, she'll read in your face.'

'A witch,' Elliot nodded solemnly. 'That explains it.'

'Oh, stop!' Sally protested self-consciously. 'I'm just interested, that's all. And you make me sound like a psychic, Ruth, when I'm only observant. Not many people are really that mysterious, you know. The signs are always there. You just have to pay attention to be a good judge of character.'

'In that case,' Elliot said seriously, 'there's someone I'd like you to meet.'

'Who's that?'

'Christie Taylor.'

'Elliot!' Ruth's voice, sharp with warning.

'I've already met her,' Sally said diffidently.

Both Ruth's and Elliot's faces reflected surprise.

'Hampton's fiancée, right?' Sally went on. 'She came to the office a couple days ago, looking for Hampton.'

'Now why would she think she could find him at my office?' Ruth asked with a vague sense of unease.

'That's what I asked her,' Sally smiled with an almost wicked satisfaction, 'but she wasn't about to be that honest.'

Elliot laughed out loud, but Ruth came back angrily, 'Now just what do you mean by that?'

Sally rolled her eyes and shook her head. 'Honestly, Ruth. You close your eyes to everything! Obviously, she was hoping to catch you and Hampton together.'

Ruth sagged against the back of her chair, thunderstruck by Sally's words and all they implied. She had never mentioned her feelings for Hampton to Sally, but she had apparently surmised them all the same, and what was worse, believed that Christie was aware of them too.

'Don't look so shocked,' Sally said. 'You just finished telling Elliot I was good at reading people, and you're my favourite subject, remember. And the easiest.' She smiled in understanding, knowing all too well the illusion Ruth harboured about being an intensely private person. 'You were in love with Hampton before you ever met him,' she went on gently, 'and after my chat with him, I knew it was a mutual affliction.'

'Your chat with him?' Ruth asked weakly.

'That first day on Market Street. The day you met him at the house, remember? He stopped afterwards at the office for your home address—so he could drop off the designs, he said, but really! The poor man was so transparent. He was kind of cute, actually; like a lovesick boy pretending to be a businessman. He asked so many questions about you he could probably write your biography. He made it sound like it was just professional interest—checking on your background, that sort of thing—but the man's cursed with an honest face. He couldn't hide the truth. And he probably can't hide it from that woman, either,' she added in a tone of caution. 'I don't know how well you know her, Ruth, but take my word for it. She's not stupid.'

'I'm no threat to Christie,' Ruth said quietly.

Elliot, silent and attentive through Sally's explanation, came suddenly to life. 'What did you think of her, Sally?'

The brown eyes shifted sideways to direct an assessing glance at Elliot, then she sighed in resignation. 'She makes me want to hang garlic around the house and carry a wooden stake in my handbag. What does that tell you?'

Elliot smiled grimly and nodded once.

'Oh, Sally,' Ruth sighed with exasperation. 'Not you, too!'

'Too?'

Elliot jabbed a thumb at his chest with a knowing nod.

Ruth blew air into her cheeks in angry frustration. 'What *is* it with you people? You must look for the worst in everybody, and that's why you see it. But you're wrong about Christie! Dead wrong! She's the victim here; the innocent victim!'

She pulled in a deep, calming breath, and felt the heat of a flush in her cheeks. Her words echoed sharply in the silence that followed, and she realised she had been shouting. 'I'm sorry,' she mumbled, 'but this whole thing is so damn backwards! Hampton and I are the ones that should want to hate her, but we're constantly defending her against everyone else.'

'She did that very well, didn't she?' Sally asked softly. 'You've got to give her credit. Not many people can get their own victims to defend them.' She frowned at the consternation on Ruth's face. 'Listen, Ruth,' she said gently, reaching out to take her hand, 'I'm sorry if I upset you; but you and Hampton have your heads in the sand if you think that woman's on the up-and-up. Everything about her is a little off-key. Even the wheelchair.'

Elliot snapped to attention in his chair and leaned forward. 'What do you mean, even the wheelchair?'

'She looks too darn healthy to be an invalid,' Sally explained. 'Besides, did you ever get a look at her legs?'

'No,' Elliot answered with a frown. 'She's always been wearing slacks or a long dress.'

'Well, she wasn't the day she came to the office. Just had an afghan across her lap, but when it slipped, I caught a glimpse of a pair of great calves. Now, I'm no doctor, but wouldn't you think useless legs would atrophy after a while? Lose their shape? I always thought paraplegics kept their legs covered because they withered, and became unattractive; but I wonder if that lady doesn't keep hers covered because they aren't.'

Elliot's smile was lopsided and positively evil. Ruth's face was totally devoid of any expression at all, but her mind was busy—frantically busy. She tried to suffocate the thought, snuff out the hope while it was still only a tiny flame, before it burst into a roaring, consuming conflagration.

Of course you'd love to believe Christie was a fake, she admonished herself sternly. That would be perfect, and oh, so convenient. She keeps you and Hampton apart, so you want her to be evil, right? And if she is, then he would be free, and that's why you want to believe it.

She struggled with her thoughts for a long time while Elliot and Sally watched her face expectantly; waiting, she guessed, for a student they thought a trifle dim-witted to come up with the correct answer. But was it the right answer, or only a convenient one? If Sally's suspicions were true, and Elliot obviously thought they were, that meant Christie Taylor was a cold, calculating, vengeful woman; the total opposite of what Ruth and Hampton both believed her to be. She would be evil beyond understanding, sacrificing her own happiness to exact vengeance from another. And that was the flaw in the reasoning. Even if Christie hated Hampton, marrying him would be as much a punishment for her as it would be for him. That was the part that simply didn't make sense; the piece that made the whole notion fall apart.

Finally Ruth sighed and moved her head back and forth in a weary denial. 'You said it yourself, Sally,' she said tiredly. 'Christie isn't stupid. Why would she imprison herself in a marriage she didn't want? Revenge is pointless when it hurts you, too.'

'Revenge?' Sally asked blankly. 'Does she have a reason to want revenge from Hampton?'

Elliot silenced her with a quick lift of the head that said he would explain later, and Ruth was almost grateful when she saw the gesture. She had no desire to relay the long, gruesome story herself.

'You explain it, Elliot,' she said, rising wearily from the table. 'And after he does, Sally, you'll see why the whole thing just doesn't make sense.'

'Maybe we just don't know enough yet, Ruth,' Elliot said hesitantly, and then more firmly, 'but I have good reason to suspect there's a great deal more to know. Your innocent, helpless, supposedly paralysed victim made a rather audacious pass at me on the terrace last night.'

'What?' Ruth and Sally chorused together.

'Surprising, isn't it?' Elliot said drily.

Ruth's expression clouded for a moment, then cleared. 'That's not fair, Elliot. She was drunk, and if liquor gave her a few moments of oblivion from the life she's forced to lead into a life she wished she could still enjoy—well, she's got that coming. She's entitled to her fantasies. We all are.'

Sally started to say something, but Elliot pressed one finger to the back of her hand in warning.

Ruth's lips lifted in a thin, half-hearted smile. 'I'm ashamed to admit that I wanted it to be true. I wanted Christie to be a fraud. I'm not very proud of that.'

She left the room then, and felt their eyes on her back as she made her way down the hall to her bedroom. She had only been awake for an hour or two, but felt suddenly exhausted.

I'll sleep away the whole day, she thought as she slipped off her robe and climbed back in between the sheets. Her eyes closed heavily and she drifted off with surprising ease, only faintly aware of the muted murmurs of urgent conversation coming from the kitchen.

CHAPTER TEN

IT was foolish to come here on a Sunday. Without the constant noise of the workmen, Hampton House was forlorn, and strangely depressing.

As she walked through the empty, silent rooms, Ruth felt a sense of pointlessness, as if the work on this house would serve no purpose. Normally there was immense satisfaction in her work; a lingering sense of fulfilment to create an environment where people would find happiness. There was no such feeling about this house any longer. No matter how much skill and creativity went into it, no matter how perfectly the labours were executed, no one would be happy in Hampton House. Not Christie, who hated the designs, and certainly not Hampton, who hated his future. No children would ever race down these cavernous hallways, filling the hollow corridors with the echoes of delighted laughter, bringing the place alive. No joy would fill the rooms and hide the flaws with the warmth of love and family.

She touched a cold, stone wall almost tenderly, feeling suddenly sorry for the old house.

'I thought I'd find you here.'

She jumped and turned quickly, her pulse racing at the unexpected voice. 'Dammit, Elliot! You scared me half to death!'

He affected remorse with a lift of his brows and slipped an arm around her shoulders. 'What're you doing here on a Sunday, anyway? The place is like a morgue. Gives me the creeps without people in it.'

'Me, too.' She dropped her head briefly on his shoulder, then looked up at him quizzically. 'So what are you doing here?'

'Looking for you. Hampton called.'

'Oh?' she said weakly.

'He wants to see what we've done on the plans. I told him we'd meet him at the site.'

'I'll have to go home first. Pick up my sketches.'

'They're in the car.'

'Well, I should change . . .' She gestured at her faded jeans and baggy shirt, smiling feebly.

Elliot took her by the shoulders and looked down at her sternly. 'You're stalling. Are you that afraid to see him?'

'It's easier if I don't,' she mumbled, her head down.

'You're running away.'

'Maybe.'

'Well, I won't let you. If nothing else, your career depends on that man at this point, and you're not going to give that up. Not if I can help it. Besides,' he added gently, 'the worst will be over soon.'

'I'm afraid you're wrong about that,' she said sadly. 'The worst of this situation is going to last forever.'

He smiled mysteriously and chucked her under the chin. 'Oh, ye of little faith,' he intoned.

He tugged at her hand until she followed him reluctantly to his car. 'Hop in,' he ordered. 'I'll drive.'

She tried to relax, sagging against the seat and commanding slow, deep breaths, but the effort was futile. She hadn't seen Hampton since the dinner over a week before, and the prospect was unsettling. She could function, she had found, as long as nothing reminded her of what she was losing. If she didn't see Hampton or Christie, she could avoid thinking about them for a time at least, filling her mind with design specifications and crew schedules, blocking out everything else. She worked long hours at Hampton House, staying after the workmen had left, hunched over her drawing board late into the night, stumbling off to bed only when physical exhaustion demanded it. As long as there was work, she could ward off the despair. As long as she didn't see Hampton.

'How's Sally?' she asked suddenly, trying to fill the silence that let her thoughts roam dangerously free.

'Sally is wonderful,' Elliot smiled. 'I don't know how she managed to live as long as she did without me, though.'

Ruth smiled at the affected immodesty, hearing the warm affection in his voice. He had changed remarkably over the last week, and Ruth knew Sally was partly, if not totally, responsible for that. The bitterness was gone, and the aimlessness, and Elliot radiated contentment, and on occasion, brilliant flashes of pure, unadulterated joy.

'You're good for each other,' she remarked. 'And it shows. But I don't think either of you will live through the courtship with the hours you keep. Do you know you haven't been home before the wee hours one night this week? Sally will drop at her desk one day soon.'

Elliot's eyes touched her with a mischievous glint. 'So who said I was with Sally all that time?'

'You'd better have been with Sally all that time,' Ruth warned him with a scowl, 'or she'll have your head on a platter, and so will I. That's one girl you'd better not trifle with!'

'Take it easy!' he laughed. 'Sally knows where I am every minute, and exactly what I'm doing.' He nodded with a distant smile, pleased with some secret thought. 'As a matter of fact, she's engineered my every move ever since we met.'

Ruth managed a weak smile, pleased that at least one relationship was progressing just as it should.

Because she was so reluctant to arrive, the trip went quickly, and her stomach tightened into a single, hard knot of dread as they turned off the highway on to the dirt track.

She had forgotten how commanding Hampton's presence could be; or perhaps her nervous anticipation made the impact of seeing him all the greater. As they broke from the dark twists of the wooded road into the light, open meadow, his figure burst upon her vision as if he were the only object in sight, with the hill and the clouds and the sky simply background for his presence. He was dressed all in black, standing at the hill's edge like a dark vertical slash against the summer blue sky. The sun glittered in the lightness of his hair like dozens of electrical sparks, looking as if it would burst into hot yellow flames at any moment. He turned slowly when he heard the car, and Ruth pressed back deeper into the seat, feeling the impact of eyes she could barely discern from this distance. She was suddenly conscious of the most trivial things: smudged scuff marks on her Saturday tennis shoes, the faded panels on her friendly, time-worn jeans, the shapelessness of her comfortable old shirt. She would have dressed differently, had she known they would meet. For the first time in her life, she would have dressed to make an impression. To be with this man, of all the men in the world, she needed a gown, and jewellery, and hair swept high upon her head. Even in slacks and a sweater, standing there casually with his hands thrust deeply into his pockets, he made her feel like that.

'Aren't you going to get out, Ruth?' Elliot brushed gently at a wisp of hair curling in front of her ear.

'Is my ponytail straight?' she asked with a wry self-contempt totally unlike her. God! Of all days to pull her thick hair back into a juvenile tail that bounced like an hysterical appendage!

'It's perfectly straight,' Elliot said gravely, somehow understanding.

'I never told you the best part, Elliot,' she said bitterly. 'The apology he made to me the last time we were here was for interfering in our love affair. You'll be happy to know that he gave us his blessing.'

Elliot snorted. 'Empty words. If it had happened, it would have killed him.'

'I doubt it,' she said drily. 'He doesn't look like a dead man, does he?'

'You mean you didn't tell him that our relationship wasn't like that? You let him believe . . .?

'It seemed pointless to say anything one way or the other, Elliot. He was totally indifferent.'

'Really.' Elliot smiled sceptically, reaching for the door handle. 'And you actually believed that.' He shook his head disparagingly. 'Come on, Ruth. It's lesson time.'

He was out of the car before she could ask what he meant, and she followed reluctantly, wishing she could melt into the grass and become too small to be seen. Elliot waited for her at the front of the car, then slipped one arm around her shoulders, pulling her close enough to whisper in her ear, 'You look fresh, and alive, and irresistibly delectable; like a sixteen-year-old begging to be seduced.'

She smiled a little at his attempt to reassure her, and shivered at the ticklish sensation of his breath against her ear.

'What's more,' he continued in a low, hoarse whisper, 'any man alive would want to rip off those clothes to see what was making all those delicious curves.'

'Elliot!' She pulled away quickly, flushing a brilliant rose, her eyes wide with astonishment.

'I thought that might put a little colour in your cheeks,' he grinned, touching her parted lips with the tip of one finger.

She was still blushing when they walked over to Hampton, uncomfortably aware that from a distance, the exchange must have looked like the intimate teasing of two lovers. Poor, dear Elliot! Thinking he would drive Hampton to some display of jealousy, when all he was really accomplishing was a further demonstration that Ruth was everything Hampton thought she was—a fickle woman, ready and eager to hop from one bed to another.

Hampton looked directly at Elliot, matching the younger man's impudent grin with a frigid, disinterested glare. 'I hope I haven't spoiled your day,' he said coldly.

'Can't be done,' Elliot replied. He directed a passionate, meaningful glance at Ruth, and she would have laughed at his overacting if he hadn't chosen that moment to close his fingers around the back of her neck.

Her eyes widened at the unmistakably intimate touch of his hand, and her flush deepened when he reached up and tugged at her ponytail, tipping her head back and turning it towards him in one gesture. The action was distinctly possessive; the subtle statement of a man demonstrating brute power over a woman he controlled.

'Elliot . . .' she began softly, ready to beg him to stop the senseless charade.

'Later,' he interrupted fiercely; and then to Hampton, 'This won't take long, will it?'

Ruth twisted her head out of Elliot's grip in time to see Hampton's eyes flicker with an expression that registered the instantaneous control of a violent impulse, then he turned away. 'No. It shouldn't take long.'

Elliot went back to the car to retrieve the plans, leaving Ruth and Hampton standing alone. She dropped her eyes to the ground in sudden embarassment, and watched the toe of one tennis shoe scuff back and forth in the long tangled grasses.

'How are you?' he asked indifferently, looking out over the view.

'Fine,' she mumbled downward. 'And you?'

'Busy.'

She resisted as long as she could, then allowed herself to look up. There were faint creases of strain around his eyes, but his gaze was cold and implacable. 'You look tired,' she told him.

'It's been a hard week.'

Her hand twitched with the impulse to reach out and

brush back his hair, but she contained it with a great effort.

'This is very difficult,' she said finally, more to fill the strained silence than anything else.

Much to her surprise, he tipped his head back and laughed. It was a harsh, brittle sound. 'I should think it would be,' he said cryptically. 'Although it's not quite accurate to call us rivals, since one lover followed so quickly on the heels of another, I imagine seeing us together *is* a bit awkward.'

Her eyes widened and she felt her face flush a bright, angry red. Allowing him to believe that their brief encounter had been casual was one thing; letting him think she could run from his bed to Elliot's within the space of a week was another altogether. 'Now wait just one minute . . .' she began hotly, but at that point Elliot came blustering up from behind, cutting her sentence short.

'Well, well. Shall we look at these right away?' He held a long tube of rolled paper in one hand, and slipped the other around Ruth's shoulders.

She swallowed the rest of her own words in frustration, and closed her eyes. She didn't know which was worse: having Hampton believe she and Elliot were lovers, or having to admit to herself that he was truly indifferent to that knowledge.

Elliot stared directly at Hampton while his hand moved absently up and down Ruth's upper arm. It was such a casual, impersonal gesture that Ruth was surprised to note Hampton's inordinate attention to it. While Elliot continued to spout small talk about his ideas for the house, Hampton's eyes remained riveted on the motions of Elliot's hand on Ruth's arm. His face remained stonily expressionless, but a wave of colour crept up his neck until his entire face was darkened.

Hampton's eyes shifted suddenly to take in Elliot's cocky half-smile, and the arrogant slant to his heavy-lidded eyes.

It seemed to Ruth that there was an immediate, subtle alteration in the air around them, making it somehow lighter, as if an electrical charge had been released somewhere nearby. She sensed the crackling tension, and saw the silent, ominous glances the two men exchange a moment too late.

'What's the matter, Hampton?' Elliot asked snidely. 'Can't you stand watching someone else's hand move over this body?'

Ruth gasped at the pointed, outrageous question in the same instant that Hampton's well-contained rage exploded. His fist shot in a deadly, upward arc towards Elliot's chin.

That Elliot had expected the blow was beyond doubt. There was no other explanation for him being able to dodge so quickly. But prepared as he might have been, the fist grazed the side of his jaw with enough force to knock him to the ground. Ruth threw herself at Hampton as he lunged forward to fall on Elliot, shrieking for him to stop even as his hands grabbed at her arms to fling her heedlessly from his path. Only Elliot's laughter stopped him. He jerked to a halt in mid-stroke, his hands still grasping Ruth's arms, and stared down at Elliot in confusion.

The younger man lay on his back on the ground, propped up on one elbow, rubbing gingerly at his jaw while he laughed as if the whole ugly scene had only been a game.

When Elliot's laughter had subsided somewhat, he directed a wary glance at Hampton, ready still to spring upright and dodge another attack. 'He has a funny way of showing he's indifferent, Ruth,' he said wryly, then flashed her an impish smile. 'And I hope this little demonstration has convinced you the man still loves you, because I'm not anxious to risk an instant replay.' He frowned up at Hampton with a shake of his head. 'You could have broken my jaw, you know, if that fist had connected properly.'

He pulled himself up to a sitting position and wrapped his arms around his knees, taking in Hampton's tight, angry face, and Ruth's pale, drawn one. His own expression managed to make him look like a sheepish child and a bemused parent all at the same time. 'Don't look so baffled, you two,' he chided them. 'This is all very easily explained.'

Hampton's patience was wearing thinner with each passing moment, and Ruth clutched convulsively at the arm she still held when she felt the muscles tighten beneath her fingers. 'You'd better start explaining then,' he said ominously, but he relaxed slightly, and Ruth breathed a sigh of relief.

It had been the pure, mindless rage of jealousy that had shot his fist towards Elliot, and now that the threat of violence seemed under control, Ruth's heart fluttered with the realisation that Hampton could not totally obliterate his feelings. They were still there, alive and well beneath the awful indifference. That was what Elliot had set out to prove, she realised with a tender smile of gratitude towards the fallen man: that the only people she and Hampton could fool were themselves.

'Sorry to bait you like that, old man,' Elliot grinned up at Hampton, 'but if the rest of this is going to be any good at all, Ruth needed to know exactly where you stood.'

'The rest of what? What are you talking about?' Hampton demanded. 'And what gives you the right to ...' The questions piled on top of one another as Hampton leaned further towards Elliot while Ruth struggled to hold him back.

Elliot was quick to scramble to his feet and take a cautious step backwards, but a mischievous smile still played around his mouth. 'I can see that I've damaged my credibility,' he said hastily, 'so I'll immediately revert to Plan B. I doubt if you'd believe much of what I told you now anyway. It might be better if you just see for youself.'

'Elliot!' Ruth stamped her foot and almost shouted. 'What is this all about?'

His smile softened tenderly as he looked at her. 'It's about good people and bad people, Ruth; and about being able to tell the difference.' He shook his head at her as he spoke as if he were amazed at the enormity of a child's naïvité. 'And from you, Hampton,' he added with a nod and a smug smile, 'I'll expect an apology.'

'What!' came the answering bellow.

'. . . a little later, however,' he amended quickly. 'For now, restraint will do. Come on. We'll pick up Sally first, then we'll be off. It's a long drive, and we don't have a lot of time.' With that, he sprinted towards his car, taking it for granted that Ruth and Hampton would follow.

Hampton's body relaxed the moment Elliot was out of range of his confused anger, and he sagged like a puppet on slack strings. 'Do you have any idea of what's going on?' he asked tiredly, rubbing at his temple with his free hand. Ruth still clutched at his other arm, and released her grip quickly when she realised she was doing it.

'None,' she replied heavily, then pulled in a deep breath to release the tension.

They were standing so closely together that Ruth could see his chest rise and fall out of the corner of her eye without ever shifting her gaze from Elliot's distant form.

'He said he had baited me.'

Because his breath stirred the wisps of hair by her ear, she knew he was looking at her. 'Yes,' she said, and smiled a little towards where Elliot was standing next to his car, shifting his weight impatiently from one foot to the other. 'I wonder if anyone ever had such a friend before,' she mused. 'You really could have broken his jaw, you know, but he risked that, just to prove you weren't really indifferent.'

'God,' he moaned. 'How could you ever have believed that?'

She cocked her head to look him full in the eye. 'You were very convincing,' she smiled. 'Until today.'

His eyes held hers steadily, but his expression was guarded. 'And you and Elliot were even more convincing. Are you, or are you not, lovers?' He asked the question point-blank, revealing nothing of what the answer might cost him.

'Of course not,' she said gently, smiling when she saw the guard slip and relief flood his face. 'Aside from everything else, Sally would kill me.'

'Sally?' he whispered, reaching for her face and caring nothing about Sally at all.

'A lot has happened in the last week,' she murmured, closing her eyes when his lips finally touched hers.

'Come on, you two!' Elliot called, startling them both into a sudden remembrance that they had an audience. 'Follow me!'

It was such a jolly call, bright with the anticipation of a great adventure, that it held back the insistent reminders of their lives off the hill. Ruth felt a peculiar tingling in her stomach, as if a childhood friend had just called her to join in a carefree game.

'Well, what do you think?' Hampton asked with a wry smile, reaching for her hand and squeezing it lightly. 'The man's obviously an incorrigible. Do we follow him blindly, without a single idea of where he's taking us?'

'Blindly is the only way to follow Elliot,' she laughed. 'You'd have to be crazy to follow him with your eyes open.'

There was a comfortable silence between them in the car as they followed Elliot. Ruth felt an odd lightening, as if she had given up total responsibility for her life to someone else, and was being pulled along without effort, content to be under the control of another. She didn't know where Elliot was leading them, and she didn't care. The very fact that they were being led seemed to shift all responsibility for their actions to Elliot, and for the moment she was untroubled and almost carefree. Hampton must have felt the same thing, for he was as relaxed as Ruth had ever seen him.

This is the way he should always look, she thought with a tiny sigh of contentment. He drove with one hand draped over the steering wheel, the other resting lightly on the console between them. His face was clear and untroubled, and the severe line of his mouth was softened into a near smile. The telltale muscle that clenched his jaw when he was tense or struggling against emotion was still, blending smoothly into the strong lines of his profile.

'You look almost happy,' she commented, laying her head sideways against the back of the seat so she could look at him. 'I don't think I've ever seen you looking like this.'

He shook his head a little and let the smile show. 'Everything seems so right,' he said, mystified. 'It doesn't make sense, I know, because nothing has really changed.'

'I know,' she whispered. 'I feel it too.'

'Maybe it's because I failed so miserably trying to pretend I didn't love you.' He continued to look straight ahead at the road, but his free hand reached for hers. Their fingers slid easily together, as if they were meant to be intertwined. 'Loving you, admitting it, realising it will always be there—it's easier than pretending it isn't.' He closed his eyes briefly and a shadow crossed his face. 'I'm not sure how we'll live with it.'

'I don't want to think about that now,' she said, tightening her fingers around his, a frown marring the smooth plane of her forehead. 'I want to be right here, right now, looking at you, holding your hand as if I had every right to, thinking everything is as it should be. Even if it only lasts a few more minutes. When it's over, I'll think of the rest. But not yet.'

He glanced over at her quickly, an expression of indescribable tenderness reaching out from the steady grey eyes to possess her completely. He could do that, she marvelled silently. Without ever touching her, he could do that.

They stopped briefly at Sally's apartment, and obeyed with questioning reluctance when Elliot demanded that they park Hampton's car and transfer to the back seat of Sally's battered Chevy. After a short, bewildered wait, Elliot reappeared from the building's front door with Sally in tow. The two had their heads pressed together as they walked towards the car, and were obviously engaged in hurried, excited conversation.

'Hi!' Sally said brightly as she slid into the driver's seat. 'I suppose we're all a bit old for double-dating, but that's what this feels like doesn't it?'

Elliot closed the passenger door with a thud and frowned pointedly at Sally. 'Drive, woman,' he commanded sternly, softening the words with a light, affectionate caress of her cheek. She smiled meekly and obeyed.

'All right, Elliot,' Ruth said firmly as the car backed out on to the street. 'Enough is enough. What's going on?'

'Have you seen Christie this week, Hampton?' Sally interrupted oddly. Ruth caught a glimpse of the younger woman's mischievous smile in the rear view mirror.

'She's spending some time in the country with friends,' Hampton replied stiffly. The muscle was tightened again in his cheek, Ruth noted with regret, feeling the sense of ease fly away with the speed of a spent bullet.

It had all been so perfect, if only for a little while. And Sally had been right, even if her comment had been dreadfully tasteless. With the four of them in the car together, it *had* almost seemed like a double date. As if they were off on a carefree outing, with every right to be together. And then Sally had had to ask that. Bringing up Christie with an almost malicious directness, reminding them all that this was only a slice of a fairytale, and that the obligations of reality would end it soon enough.

'Where are we going?' Ruth persisted, her voice toneless and impatient.

'There's something we want you to see,' Elliot said gently, turning in his seat to smile reassuringly at them both. He had heard the brittle tension in Ruth's voice, and knew there was no tolerance left. 'It's a surprise, and you'll both make us very happy if you can wait just a bit longer. Besides, I love a good mystery, don't you?'

Ruth glared a warning at him, and was puzzled by Hampton's apparent complacence. She expected him to be every bit as irritated with this nonsensical charade as she was, but instead his eyes met Elliot's with a curious, almost amused assessment, and he said nothing.

They rode in silence for a time, and Ruth barely noticed Hampton's hand reaching over to cover hers, she was so intent on the route they were following. The freeway led south from the city, breezing by the huddled collections of outskirt motels and truck stops, stretching finally into the gentle, rolling hills of freshly turned cropland.

'This is the Suburban Motel,' Elliot said suddenly, indicating a sprawling complex of individual bungalows that whizzed by on their left. 'The management has a reputation for discretion, and more illicit affairs take place within those walls than any other spot near the city.'

Ruth bit down on an indignant response. Perhaps she was being too sensitive. Perhaps that's why it sounded as if Elliot was suggesting a place for her and Hampton to carry on an affair after his marriage. But what other reason could he have had for pointing out such an establishment? She slumped further down into the seat, feeling suddenly tawdry and guilty, as though she had already participated in the adulterous liaison Elliot was suggesting. She risked a sideways glance at Hampton, and saw that his lips were pressed together in a thin, white line. He, too, was holding back a response.

'Sally's going to propose to me soon,' Elliot said unexpectedly, his voice lightening, taking on a teasing tone.

'I most certainly am not!' Sally retorted. 'I've only known you a week.'

'I'm surprised you've managed to hold out this long,' he grinned. 'And if you think The Summit's something,' he continued to Ruth and Hampton, 'wait until you see the house I'll design for us. You will do the interior, won't you, Ruth?'

So that was it! Ruth felt relief mingle with an odd disappointment. Even though it might seem sudden to anyone else, it came as no surprise to her that Sally and Elliot had decided so quickly to marry. And now they had chosen a homesite, and that was what they were going to see.

'Of course I will,' she answered quickly, leaning forward in the seat, trying to muster the excitement she wanted to feel for her two friends. It was just so blasted difficult, to generate happiness for everyone else's wedding.

Hampton was shaking his head with a rare smile. 'This is a little too sudden for me,' he chuckled. 'I've gone from thinking Elliot was sleeping with Ruth to Elliot marrying Sally, all in the space of an hour or so.'

'What?' Sally shrieked.

'Never mind,' Elliot reassured her with a low laugh. 'I'll tell you later. I slipped a quick second act into the master plan.'

Ruth pursed her lips in exasperation, thoroughly confused by Elliot's comment, and about to demand an explanation when Sally angled off on to a narrow tar road leading into the hills.

'This is Hillshire,' she explained in a curt, businesslike

tone. 'You've heard of it, of course. A quaint little resort town with lovely shops, great scenery, and private cottages by the lake.'

As if on cue the little town appeared in a shallow valley below, nestled in the surrounding forest like a picturesque postcard. It was lovely enough, Ruth thought, but no match for the breath-stopping views from the river bluffs where Elliot's current house stood. She couldn't imagine Elliot trading that scenery for this.

'Let's stop for some lunch,' Sally said as she pulled into the parking lot of one of those glass-and-steel restaurants that look more in place at freeway rest stops than in the middle of an old town's venerable brick structures.

Hampton shrugged at Ruth with a resigned expression. Elliot and Sally were already out of the car, and it was obvious that they had no intention of waiting for their passengers' approval of the luncheon idea.

The hostess greeted Elliot with familiarity, and Ruth imagined that he must have eaten here when shopping for a homesite on earlier trips. Elliot insisted on a booth at the back of the restaurant, far from the large front windows, shielded from the rest of the room by a tall, ugly planter of latticed wood.

'Really, Elliot,' she complained, 'couldn't we take that table by the window so I can at least see the town? I can barely find my seat back here, it's so dark.'

'Sally and I sat at this very table only yesterday,' Elliot responded with a mysterious smile, 'and I can guarantee that the view from here is the best in the place.'

In point of fact, the view became absolutely irrelevant when Hampton slipped into the booth beside her and reached under the table for her hand.

After they had ordered, Elliot and Sally exchanged a meaningful glance before Elliot leaned across the table towards them, braced on his arms. 'All right,' he said firmly, with all the light and laughter gone from his voice and his eyes. 'We have fifteen minutes as I time it, and there are a few things I think you should know first.' He spoke quickly, before either of them had a chance to ask what would happen in fifteen minutes. 'Hampton, did you know that Christie's family is virtually penniless?' He directed a steady, inescapable stare towards Hampton's suspicious frown.

The totally unexpected question, and the demanding tone in which it was delivered, caught Hampton off-guard. For that reason, and that alone, he answered without thinking. 'That's ridiculous! Aside from the fact that the Taylors are quite wealthy independently, the insurance settlement after the accident was enormous. The returns on that investment alone must be a small fortune by now.' His face tightened and closed suddenly, and his eyes darkened with suspicion, but before he could chastise Elliot for asking questions which were none of his business, Ruth intervened with an angry hiss.

'Elliot, if this has anything to do with your ridiculous suspicions about Christie, stop right now! I don't want to hear another word!'

'What suspicions?' Hampton demanded. 'What the hell is going on here?'

'Suspicions that Christie is not the self-sacrificing saint you both believe she is,' Elliot said smoothly, leaning back in his chair. Sally's gaze flickered warily from Hampton to Ruth, and she laid a protective hand on Elliot's arm as if to say she would defend him against any attack.

'Her father's money was nearly gone as long ago as the night of her coming out party,' Elliot continued blithely. 'Bad investments, overindulgence, and an unfortunate penchant for gambling wiped out the family fortune when Christie was still a teenager. A good, solid marriage of convenience would have bailed the family out at that point, but the accident destroyed any hope of that. All of a sudden, Christie wasn't the catch of the county anymore.'

Ruth looked quickly at Hampton, and trembled when she saw the dangerous rush of dark colour to his face, the tight lines of rage around his eyes. Elliot should have known better, she thought tensely, then to bring up the accident. Any more of this, and Hampton would explode, with very good reason.

Elliot went on in an unconcerned voice, although he never took his eyes off Hampton, as if he were well aware of the rage he was courting. 'Fortunately, the accident settlement came just in time to spare the family financial embarassment, and they managed to keep up appearances quite nicely for a time.' He paused significantly and levelled a pointed glance at Hampton. 'And then Christie's parents died.'

Hampton's mouth dropped open and his eyes flew wide. Ruth's face was a duplicate image.

'That's right,' Elliot nodded, satisfied with their reaction. 'Her parents have been dead for years—died in a car crash on one of those dreadful Swiss roads. But she never bothered to mention that, did she? Small wonder. As long as you thought they were still alive and holding the grudge that kept you at a distance, you'd stay put in the States and she'd have Europe all to herself.'

Hampton's eyes had the dull, glazed appearance of someone who had just been asked to believe the impossible. 'I don't understand,' he mumbled. 'I visited her in Europe often. I would have known . . .'

'Twice a year,' Sally contributed. 'With plenty of advance notice, and only at the hospital when she was in for treatment. And that much was true, of course. She did have a lot of dreadful operations, but for the last several years, they've only been cosmetic. Like any other woman who goes in for a facelift. And she only stayed for a week at a time, not months, as she led you to believe.'

Hampton's head was moving back and forth in the regular, methodical motions of shock. Ruth squeezed his hand lightly. 'Why?' The word escaped his lips with this hiss of expended breath. 'Why would she want me away from Europe? Why did she lie?'

'Because she was very busy,' Elliot snapped, but Sally frowned a warning and tipped a compassionate head towards Hampton.

'The money ran out, Hampton,' she said gently. 'It had to, eventually. She's been living like royalty on it for years. The well finally ran dry, and that's when she agreed to set a wedding date. She needs the Hampton wealth. A quick wedding, then a quick divorce, and any American judge would be happy to award Jonathan Hampton's pathetic, crippled wife whatever she asked. She'd be set for life.'

There was a long, dead silence at the table while Ruth and Hampton tried to absorb it all, then Hampton spoke with empty finality. 'Even if everything you say is true, it changes nothing. If she's marrying me only for money, so be it. I owe her that. But it doesn't mean she's premeditating divorce. You're wrong about that.'

That was it. Ruth sat bolt upright in her seat when it all come together with the deafening impact of a clap of thunder in her mind. The reason Christie would marry Hampton, even if she hated him; the reason she had first looked for last weekend when Sally had voiced her suspicions about Christie being crippled at all. It was the money. Something as simple as that, and so obvious that she had never thought of it. A quick marriage, with no risk of a distasteful consummation since Hampton thought she was incapable of it; then an equally quick divorce. She would get everything she wanted from Hampton, without tying herself down.

'How do you know all this?' she asked suddenly, her eyes overly bright and riveted on Elliot.

Elliot smiled slowly, his brows lifted to a pleased arch when he saw Ruth's expression. Then his eyes darted to the side and he sobered suddenly, dropping his voice to a whisper. 'Later,' he hissed urgently. 'We'll explain it all. For now, don't say a word, either of you. Just turn around slowly, and look towards the door.'

They both did as they were told. Ruth felt Hampton's hand close convulsively around hers, and they both jerked back at the same time, as if they had been struck an identical blow.

'Dear God,' Ruth whispered, feeling nothing through the shock as much as an enormous sense of betrayal.

The woman walked through the front doorway towards a tall, rail-thin man waiting for her by the entrance. Her step was quick and sure, her chin tilted upward to direct a fleeting smile. When she reached the man, she raised on tiptoes to accept the man's light peck on her cheek, then they walked together to a small table by the window. If anything, Christie was more beautiful standing and in motion than she had been immobile in a wheelchair.

Ruth had to concentrate to force the mechanical motions required for breathing. Even from this distance, and through the dulling shock of seeing Christie walk with no effort whatsoever, the striking resemblance between the two people she was watching registered in some distant recess of Ruth's mind.

'That's her brother,' Elliot whispered, and Ruth saw Hampton's head bob once in astounded affirmation. 'The papers they're examining so carefully are Christie's divorce papers,' Elliot continued. 'The waitress here was too nosy not to notice, and too greedy not to tell when I offered a remarkably healthy tip. They've been meeting here every day this week to work on them. And though the waitress is no literary giant, she is, at least, literate. Your name is on those papers, Hampton. They outline her divorce settlement from you.'

A dozen questions raced through her mind without stopping, and Ruth ignored them all for the moment. She continued to stare without blinking through the planter's latticework at what fascinated her most of all:

Christie's legs. They were beautifully shaped, well-toned, crossed to one side in an alluring, habitual pose, and Ruth couldn't pull her eyes away. She didn't notice Hampton's hand sliding away from hers, or the terrifying look of rage that consumed his features and made his face frightening. Nor did she notice when the expression altered suddenly and became something else. By the time she turned to look at him, his features were placid and composed, and amazingly, the beginnings of a smile tugged at his mouth.

'Excuse me,' he said quietly, and rose from the booth.

'Not a chance,' Elliot stopped him with a hand on his arm. 'Everyone at this table deserves to see this. We go together.'

'No,' Ruth said quickly, looking down at her lap. 'Not me. I don't understand any of this, and I don't think I want to.' She raised her eyes reluctantly, and Hampton frowned at the emerald plea shining through the beginnings of tears.

'You have to, Ruth,' he said gently, touching her cheek with the tips of two fingers. 'Or you'll remember her just as she was: pathetic, helpless, tied to a chair. You have to see her as she really is. We both do.'

He pulled her gently to her feet, then they led the way across the room, Elliot and Sally close behind.

Marching, Ruth thought dully. We're all marching together towards that woman, closing in on her like a gang of cut-throats, and I don't want to be part of it. She was horrified that she might burst into tears at any moment, because she didn't know anymore, who were the good guys and who were the bad guys. It was all jumbled together in a hideous mire of pretence and betrayal, and she couldn't sort it all out. But it was coming closer and closer with every step she took, and there was no turning back, no running away from it, because now Christie had sensed that the quiet group was coming towards her, and she was looking up from the papers, her lovely face still reflecting a smile at the last thing her brother had said. Then shock crossed the face and Ruth could see the blood drain away, leaving a sheet of pallid white to frame blue eyes widened enormously, until a ring of white showed around each iris.

Then dismay, despair, fear, and a cold, implacable fury darted in quick succession across the ghostly white face, which settled finally into an expression of twisted, blinding hatred. It was a very ugly face, pinched and drawn and hating so much, and Ruth wondered how she ever could have thought it beautiful.

CHAPTER ELEVEN

'HELLO, Christie.' Hampton's words fell on the silence like hammer blows.

Christie stared at him fixedly for a long moment, then her eyes flicked with cold disdain over Ruth, Elliot, and Sally, each in turn. It had only been the briefest of glances, but it made Ruth's stomach lurch with its coldness.

A dispassionate, frightening smile twisted Hampton's lips as he glanced down at the papers spread across the table. He looked totally in control, but there was something in his eyes that made Ruth want to grab his arm and pull him away. That same something made her equally afraid to do just that.

'I don't think you'll be needing these,' Hampton said casually, sweeping the documents into a hasty pile and picking them up. With the terrible smile still fixed in place, he ripped the papers with a violent, savage gesture that startled them all. Even Christie flinched. For an instant, Ruth thought she saw fear in the flashing blue eyes, but then they narrowed to vicious slits and spewed hatred.

'You ... owe ... me ...' Christie hissed under her breath, as if each word were an arrow released towards Hampton's face.

'For what?' he asked flatly.

'For a year of my life!' she spat. 'A year in and out of hospitals! In and out of surgery! In and out of that damn chair!'

'A year?' he whispered in amazed disbelief, shock immediately displacing the towering rage that had held him erect. 'One ... year ...?'

It started as a low, strangled chuckle, that terrible

sound in his throat, but it faded quickly, like a thought too painful to complete.

'That's all it took, Hampton,' Elliot said steadily from behind him. 'Within one year her face was repaired and she was back on her feet. Her surgeon calls it his most satisfying work. He's very proud of it, actually. Loves to talk about it, especially when a fellow doctor makes a transatlantic call to stroke him a little.'

'You!' Christie hissed, flashing a venomous glare at Elliot.

'Me,' he nodded. 'Dr Elliot Shore, Dective Elliot Shore, whatever label you like. I've used them all this past week.'

'But I visited you in the hospital—twice a year—all those years ... you were always bandaged, always bedridden ...'

Ruth could hear the strength seeping out of Hampton with his words. The enormity of the betrayal was almost incomprehensible to him, and his defensive façade was crumbling quickly. She watched with sick astonishment as Christie's face reflected sadistic pleasure in seeing his wounded disbelief.

'Touch ups, for the first few years,' Elliot cut in sharply. 'Voluntary, almost to the last one. After that, it was simply cosmetic surgery, or a short hospital stay for a case of "nerves". The jet set is extremely prone to nerve problems, Hampton. Did you know that?'

Christie's brother, stonily silent up to that point, suddenly came to life. He rose to his full height and leaned his hands on the table. His face was a violent red, and Ruth noticed a persistent, nervous tic in his right eye. 'You have no right!' he bellowed, but Elliot silenced him with a pointed, accusing finger.

'Sit down, Taylor!' he barked. 'You can be disbarred in this state for a fraud conviction. And that is the very least of what this will cost you!'

The man seemed to shrivel back into himself, and sank slowly to his chair.

'Why?' Hampton asked lifelessly, his gaze on Christie.

'Why should I tell you anything!' she challenged him.

'Because fraud is a crime,' Elliot said coldly, 'and the truth is the only thing you've got to bargain with.'

She measured Elliot with a contemptuous glare, then shrugged nonchalantly. 'For the obvious reasons,' she said flatly, directing her answer to Hampton. 'I hated you passionately for the first few months. The only fun I had was watching through the bandages while you writhed with guilt. Fortunately, my jaw was wired shut long enough to keep my sentiments private. By the time I could talk, you were already full of the Sir Galahad role, determined to devote your life to me. Such a touching sacrifice!' Her laughter didn't trill the way Ruth remembered it. It cut the air with a shattering, discordant sound. 'But it *was* a sacrifice, wasn't it, Tray? Throwing your life away for a woman you didn't love? And I loved watching you suffer with it.' Her smile was thoroughly malicious. 'I really thought we would be done with it when we moved to Switzerland, but when you insisted on the twice-yearly visits . . .' She shrugged coldly. '. . . I decided why not? Why not let you think I was still suffering? It made your guilt all the worse, and you deserved it. And it didn't cost me anything. At that point I was still going in every six months for touch-up surgery, and it was easy to co-ordinate your visits for the same time. It was just a game, Tray. A small repayment for the year in hell you gave me.' Her eyes flashed with bitter satisfaction.

'A game?' Hampton breathed, moving his head back and forth in slow motion. Then his eyes closed in remembered anguish, and his words came out flat and dead. 'My God. All those years.'

Christie sniffed in a derisive chuckle. 'But the game stopped being a game when the money started to run out,' she continued bitterly. 'Then deceiving you became a necessity, and the marriage you'd been talking about all those years looked like the only way out. It was a dismal prospect, I grant you, but Andrew here,' she nodded towards her brother, 'assured me it would only be a temporary inconvenience. Then I could be on my merry way with half of your wonderful money, and probably, an income for life.'

She rolled her eyes dramatically, and broke into laughter when they came to rest on Ruth, 'Honestly, Ruth! What a naïve, silly creature you are! You look so very righteously amazed, as if I were positively evil! Believe me, it was the only thing I could do.' There was an almost merry lilt to her tone, and Ruth realised for the very first time that Christie felt absolutely no guilt for the hoax she had perpetrated all these years.

'Tray would never had married me if he hadn't felt guilty—I'm not his type at all, you see. A bit too flighty, I think he'd say. And it's not like he would have missed the money. He has buckets, you know. Positively buckets.'

Ruth found it impossible to react. Her face was frozen into a mask of pale, rigid disbelief, and her eyes were two dull circles of green that contemplated Christie with an emotion that wavered between fear and revulsion.

'Let's go,' Sally said softly from behind her, watching Ruth carefully.

Without another word, Hampton turned Ruth away from the table and started for the door. Christie's brittle laughter followed them. It was only Ruth who thought she heard the sound rise into hysterical sobs as the door hissed shut behind them.

'I liked her,' she whispered as she slipped numbly into the back seat. 'I actually liked her.'

'There was a lot to like in what she let us see,' Hampton said kindly. 'Or at least a lot to admire. We're just lucky we had friends who could see through to the other side.'

The scene with Christie had been brief, and

unpleasantly civilised. It should have been loud, and
violent, and filled with flying dishes and screaming
epithets. The only thing worse than Christie's heartless
use of Hampton was her absolute indifference to the
suffering she had caused, her ability to discuss it coolly,
calmly, without a trace of remorse. Ruth hadn't known
such callousness existed in the world.

Elliot was turned sideways in the front seat, his eyes
on Ruth with concern. 'It was brutal, wasn't it?' he
asked gently. 'For both of you.'

Neither Ruth nor Hampton made a reply. They both
sat rigidly erect, facing forward, their expressions empty
and flat.

Elliot motioned for Sally to start driving, and
turned even more in the front seat so he faced them
directly.

'It's over,' he said with a stern frown, 'unless you
both insist on ruining your lives by dwelling on it. So
you found out the fairy princess is a witch, and some of
the saints are sinners. So what? The world's full of
them, and always has been. Fortunately, there are more
good guys than bad around, and when you two start
raising your own little brood, the odds will go even
higher.'

Ruth's eyes connected with Elliot's, and the cloud
hanging over her began to lift. It was the one thing she
hadn't thought of until that moment: that Hampton
was free. She had been so obsessed with the horror of
the years he had seen wasted, that she had forgotten to
consider the endless years that stretched ahead.

'Oh my,' she said foolishly, and turned quickly to
look at him. His eyes were fixed on a point far in the
distance, and he was smiling.

'How did you do it, Elliot?' he asked quietly.

The younger man's features relaxed slightly and he
settled more comfortably into his seat. 'Simple. We
followed her,' he answered, shrugging off the importance of what had been done. 'Watched her hotel

until she left in a taxi one day early this week—still in a wheelchair, you understand—and then tailed her to the Suburban Motel. An hour after she had been wheeled into her bungalow, she *walked* out, and hopped into her brother's waiting car, agile as you please.' He broke off to laugh. 'Sally and I could barely keep from screaming out loud when we saw that. We never dreamed it would be that easy. But she was confident in your trusting nature, Hampton. I'm sure it never occurred to her that you would have had her followed, so she got careless. The rest was a piece of cake.'

Sally picked up the thread of the explanation. 'She leased a cottage in Hillshire so she had a place to escape to whenever the handicap charade became tiresome. Aside from giving her a hideaway where she could be herself, it provided a place where she and her brother could meet. He's a lawyer, you know, and was part of the scheme from the very start. No doubt she promised him a pretty healthy cut of the divorce settlement.'

'There's something else you should know, Hampton,' Elliot put in somberly. 'Although Christie probably *did* go through hell for that first year, it didn't last long, and the dividends were nothing to sneeze at. She was out of the wheelchair by the time her broken legs healed, and her face was almost totally normal after the first year. And still beautiful enough to enchant every available suitor in Europe. She lived mighty high for years on the insurance settlement, hopping in and out of affairs with any number of willing young men, including one of the doctors who treated her. She married him, although it didn't last long. And she gave him a child. He lives in France now, with the father.'

Ruth heard the faint rush of air escape Hampton's lips.

'So,' Elliot continued with a tip of his head, 'you can stop torturing yourself about having made her suffer. You were the victim here. You took fifteen years of agony compared to her one. I'd say the debt was paid in full.'

No one said anything for a moment, then Hampton leaned forward in his seat and looked Elliot directly in the eye. 'Thank you,' he said simply, and Ruth couldn't ever remember hearing two words that sounded more profound.

'Don't mention it,' Elliot replied, and although he meant it, Hampton shook his head.

'I have to mention it. How do you thank someone for giving you back your life?'

'By living it,' Elliot answered.

CHAPTER TWELVE

By the time they arrived back at the hill, the sun had begun its lingering descent to the valley floor. They had barely spoken since dropping off Sally and Elliot, and it never occurred to Ruth that this was unusual.

She had sat in silent acquiescence in the car when Hampton made a brief stop at a battered, run-down delicatessen, and had only smiled faintly when he emerged from the store carrying a large wicker hamper. It didn't surprise her that he should have been able to procure such a basket from such an unlikely store; and she never questioned his intention or their destination during the long drive afterwards. They were going to have a picnic, and it would take place on the hill. What could be more natural than that?

He spread a brightly checkered blanket on the grass while she stood watching, then knelt to unpack the hamper. Like a magician's hat, the container produced a seemingly endless variety of foods; then remarkably, a dusty bottle of champagne. When he had finished laying the spread, he leaned back on his heels and looked up at her with a boyish grin. Then his smile faded as he stared at her.

'You look like a madonna, standing there,' he said softly. His voice barely carried over the whisper of wind in the trees.

'A madonna with a ponytail?' she asked sceptically.

The boyish grin returned, dancing across his face with a silent laughter that touched his eyes. She had never seen him look quite like that before. He spread his arms wide, indicating the blanket and the bounty it held. 'This is all part of a seduction, you know. I intend to feed you until you're lazy and complacent, ply you with wine until you're helpless, then have my way with you.'

She cocked her head and looked down at him with a serious expression. 'I don't suppose you'd care to reverse the order of that plan?'

'You have absolutely no shame.'

'I think I've heard that before.'

His face clouded as a thought crossed his mind. He pushed himself to his feet by pressing his hands against his knees, then indicated that she should sit on the blanket. She complied willingly and sank to a lotus position, then looked up expectantly.

'We've never talked,' he said somberly, turning to look out over the edge of the hill.

'It never seemed necessary,' she said. 'The important things never needed saying, and the rest . . . well, it was unimportant.'

He turned his head slightly and looked down at her tenderly. 'You don't know a thing about me, Ruth. Not where I live, or what my businesses are, or what my family is like, or . . .'

'Hampton,' she interrupted him gently. 'There's nothing about you I need to know that I didn't know right from the start . . . from the first time I saw your handwriting.'

'That's a ridiculous way to fall in love with a man,' he chided her. 'You should do a little more research than that.'

She blew air out through her lips, then braced an elbow on her knee, cupping her chin in her palm. 'All right, then. I'll conduct an interview. You don't beat small children, do you?'

'No,' he grinned. 'I love children.'

'And you don't beat women?'

The grin broadened. 'Hardly ever.'

'And I already know you don't chew with your mouth full. So what else is there?' She cocked her head until her ponytail hung at a crazy angle, and looked up at him earnestly until he laughed out loud.

'Absolutely nothing, I suppose.' He lifted his shoulders in a helpless shrug and sank down on the blanket next to her. He folded his knees into an identical lotus position and faced her squarely.

'We'll be married, of course,' he said, looking directly into her eyes.

'Of course.'

'Next weekend.'

'Fine.'

'And we'll live here, in The Summit, after it's finished.'

She nodded, smiling.

'Where should we live until then?'

She giggled a little and shrugged.

'You're not taking this seriously, Ruth,' he scolded.

She rolled forward on to her knees and cupped his face in her hands. 'You're talking to whither-thou-goest Ruth, remember?' she reminded him gently. 'I can't think of anything less serious than where we're going to live.' Her eyes probed his intently and a tiny line creased her brow. 'Is the guilt gone, Hampton?'

He paused just long enough to give the word import. 'Yes.'

'Will you be bitter because so many years were wasted?'

He smiled slowly. 'I don't look at it that way. I think more of it as the rest of my life being saved. Besides, a very wise man said once that if you regret what has passed before, you must also regret where you are, because one leads to the other. And I am exactly where I want to be.'

She let both thumbs stray to the corners of his mouth. 'You sound just like Martin,' she mused.

His eyes widened in sudden recollection. 'Martin! I nearly forgot.'

He stretched out one arm to reach the hamper and pulled a bulky envelope from its depths. 'Here. Elliot said I should give this to you.'

'This?' She took the envelope and examined it briefly before tossing it aside. 'It's just the list of wines Martin left me. I picked it up at the bank after that first night at my apartment. You asked to see it then, remember? I haven't even opened it yet.'

'Elliot did. He said there was another envelope inside besides the list. He thought it might be important.'

'Another envelope?' She snatched it from the blanket and pulled out the smaller envelope inside, and her expression softened when she saw her name inscribed on it in a spidery, elegant hand. 'It's from Martin,' she whispered, and felt a catch building in her throat. She started to read it herself, but her eyes blurred with tears that Hampton kept brushing away. Finally he took the single sheet from her and began to read aloud.

My dear Ruth,

There is nothing I could leave you that would match what you gave me while I lived. If I willed you Westchester Design, Harold would only contest the bequest, and would probably win. He is, after all, my natural child, although the admission sometimes pains me.

Before you came into my life I had one all-consuming passion: my wine collection. With you as a more meaningful distraction, I have contributed little to it within the last few years, but my earlier investments have been proven sound, and as you can see from the list, the cellar is quite substantial. Harold need never know that the monetary value of this bequest is worth at least twice the total assets of Westchester. He always thought it a rather tiresome hobby; the slightly senile preoccupation of a lonely old man.

One day you may need the monetary support these wines can provide, but my fondest hope is that you will not. Each bottle is a celebration: of the bounty of nature, the reverence of age, and the harvest of history. It was meant to be drunk, and shared, and enjoyed—not hoarded as I have done.

We drank a few bottles together, Ruth. You tossed it back like grape juice, and I savoured it slowly, for every one of those occasions was a celebration for me; a celebration that you were in my life.

Think of me when you open a bottle. Know that you made an old man's last years the most meaningful of his life. And celebrate often. In the dim perspective of my later years, I finally learned that *that* was what it was all about.

Love, Martin

P.S. For God's sake, drink this with someone who has the sense to appreciate the value of a good wine!

She couldn't stop the tears. She sat perfectly still on the blanket, and never made a sound, but the tears ran freely down her cheeks and dripped from the edge of her chin to her lap. Eventually the flow subsided, and Hampton handed her a handerchief. His face was tight with the stiff look of control men wear when they're trying not to cry.

'I will regret until the day I die that I never knew that man,' he murmured, and had there been no other reason, simply for saying that, she would have loved him forever.

She extended her arms wordlessly, and he moved quickly to wrap her in an embrace that said more than any physical contact they had had. It was full of caring, and warmth, and comfort, and she sensed intuitively that this would always be there, long after the heated passions of youth had flared.

She had a sudden image of them both years in the future: white-haired, slow-moving, a little stiff with extreme age, sitting before a banking fire, nodding at the memories of a lifetime. She looked at his smooth features, the bright light of eyes promising the future, and the image and the reality blended and made her smile. 'We have to save one bottle,' she said. 'Until we're very, very old.'

He eased her down until she was lying across his lap and began stroking stray wisps of hair away from her face, cherishing her with his eyes. His fingers moved across her forehead, smoothing her brows, then followed the line of her nose down to her lips. His touch was indescribably tender, almost reverent; and she felt that all the love that was in him was flowing through the pathway of his fingertips into her soul, joining them irrevocably in a spiritual communion.

When her lips parted under his touch, releasing the hot, sweet breath of anticipation to caress his fingertips, his breath jerked to a stop and he closed his eyes. When he finally exhaled and his lids opened slowly, there was no indication that the tide of passion was sweeping him away. His gaze was steady, and dark, and a tiny smile touched the corners of his mouth. She lay there in his arm, her eyes wide with wonder at the power of desire building within her, shuddering when he began releasing the buttons of her shirt. His hand pressed against the flat of her stomach while he bent to touch the peak of each breast with the tip of his tongue, and she felt the air leave her body in a sudden rush.

He lifted his head long enough to look directly into her eyes, but his hand continued the gentle pressure on her stomach. 'Are you hungry?' he asked huskily, jerking his head in a brusque gesture to indicate all the food.

Her eyes brightened mischievously. 'Yes,' she whispered.

His hand slid downward from her stomach and she caught her breath.

'No,' she amended quickly, and his smile widened.

Harlequin Presents

Coming Next Month

ATTRACTIVE, SPACE SAVING BOOK RACK

Display your most prized novels on this handsome and sturdy book rack. The hand-rubbed walnut finish will blend into your library decor with quiet elegance, providing a practical organizer for your favorite hard-or soft-covered books.

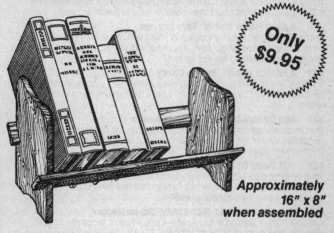

Only $9.95

Approximately 16" x 8" when assembled

Assembles in seconds!

To order, rush your name, address and zip code, along with a check or money order for $10.70 ($9.95 plus 75¢ postage and handling) (New York residents add appropriate sales tax), payable to *Harlequin Reader Service* to:

In the U.S.

Harlequin Reader Service
Book Rack Offer
901 Fuhrmann Blvd.
P.O. Box 1325
Buffalo, NY 14269-1325

Offer not available in Canada.

BKR-1